NO. 13
TORONI

NO.13
TORONI

NO. 13 TORONI

JULIUS REGIS

A Mystery

WILDSIDE PRESS

Originally published in 1922.
Published by Wildside Press, LLC
Visit us online at wildsidepress.com.

INTRODUCTION

KARL WURF

Julius Regis (1889–1925) was a Swedish writer and journalist whose quick, popular mysteries helped shape early Scandinavian crime fiction. He was born and died in Stockholm, and he worked in newspapers and became a pioneer of film journalism before turning to fast-moving fiction. His best-known creation is Maurice Wallion—a reporter-detective nicknamed "the Problem Hunter"—who anchors several novels and stories.

In the 1920s, European crime stories were moving from the refined puzzle model toward livelier, press-room realism. Contemporary reviewers compared Maurice Wallion—lightly—to Sherlock Holmes, but stress he is not a copy. Regis favored reportage, momentum, and modern settings over pure armchair detection. That blend places him between the classic British riddle mystery and the later, socially aware Swedish school that would emerge decades after his death.

The Wallion tales show a journalist's eye: short, vivid scenes; clear stakes; practical clues; and professional networks that pull a reporter into danger. Regis's newspaper background and film columns likely fed his brisk pacing and visual style, which suited readers of "entertainments" in the post-World War I era.

Regis also wrote early science-adventure fiction. In recent years, scholars have recovered his Martian epics from Swedish magazines, showing him in dialogue with Jules Verne and set alongside H.G. Wells, George Griffith, Edwin Lester Arnold, and Edgar Rice Burroughs. Even in the science fction, thoughs, his instinct is journalistic: observe, describe, move. Those influences matter because they explain the forward thrust and curiosity that animate his crime novels.

No. 13 Toroni (the novel in your hands) was among the first of his books to appear in English, published in New York by Henry Holt in 1922. It features Wallion in another intricate case told with pace and clarity, characteristic of Regis's approach to the mystery form. The book's English-language presence today owes much to library holdings and public-domain access, which have preserved its text for new readers.

If you enjoy this novel's tone and method, seek out other Regis titles featuring Maurice Wallion: *The Copper House* (1923, also available from Wildside Press) offers a tightly built, clue-driven investigation. I am aware of two other, later titles, though I have never read them. *The Blue Track* reportedly shows Wallion in a brisk, continental pursuit; and *Der Mann vom Meer* (which tranlates as "The Man from the Sea") presents a coastal mystery.

PART I

THE MYSTERY OF ELAINE ROBERTSON

CHAPTER 1

STEPS THAT GROW SILENT

"They are all gone ... all, that crazy Craig Russel, Sanderson, the black Colonel, all gone. All, save William Robertson, myself and you, and the mystery of King Solomon is not solved...."

Victor Dreyel left off writing and looked expectantly towards the door. As he sat there in his well-lighted studio he looked rather like an old bird of prey in a glass cage. All round him reigned unbroken silence, but in his clear, sad eyes there lurked an expression of suspense, and, if any of his fellow-lodgers in No. 30 John Street had seen him at that moment, they would have said he had cause for the strain; he had the look of one suffering from painful memories.

Victor Dreyel, a silent man of about sixty, with wrinkled face and white hair well brushed back from his forehead, his light blue eyes shaded by bushy brows, was spare and thin. Fifteen years ago, when first he had taken up his abode on the fifth floor of No. 30 John Street, in one of the oldest and least frequented quarters of Stockholm, he had been an object of much curiosity among the neighbors; he seemed so lonely, so reticent, yet well able to shift for himself, and as he refused all offers of help with cool but studied politeness, some sort of story regarding his former life had to be invented and set going. One heard that he had been mixed up with Chinese smugglers on the coast of California, another was informed that he had taken part in some Arctic expedition which had ended disastrously; the general opinion, however, was that he had led a life of adventure and had returned to Sweden from North America, where he had been implicated in some mysterious affair which had left an indelible mark upon his character.

His business in No. 30 John Street was a very prosaic one—he set up as a photographer. He was fairly capable though, occasionally, a little behind the times. A showcase outside the front door which bore witness to his skill, might have attracted a goodly number of customers, had not the Gothic brick walls of St. John's Church and a thick clump of trees cut John Street off from all ordinary traffic, so that with the years, Dreyel's studio became more and more desolate and empty. People left off associating the aged photographer, in threadbare but well-brushed garments, with any exciting adventure; and there came a time when his very existence was forgotten. For fifteen years the silent lodger went in and out of the old house like a stranger, people got accustomed to him, though the secret of his life had never been discovered.

It was, however, decreed that the interest of Victor Dreyel's neighbors should be aroused once more, and that in a way no one would have dreamed of, on the evening of the first of August, 1918....

After having again cast wistful glances at the door, Dreyel once more bent over his desk and continued to write: "Fifteen years have I been living in this somber and quiet corner; perhaps it was my time of probation all along. They say likenesses of the dead bring misfortune to the living. After all those years it was a curious gift to you and me; and whatever may happen tonight I shall not give in without a struggle...."

Suddenly he let his pen fall. The church clock struck eight and at the same moment there was a sharp ring at the door. Dreyel's face grew hard and alert; he passed through the studio and waiting-room, and opened the door into the passage; a young man in dripping rain-coat entered precipitately.

"You have been a long time, Murner," said Dreyel. "Have you brought him with you?"

"No, he is coming at nine o'clock," replied the young man, throwing his hat upon a chair, "he couldn't come earlier. I had a good deal of trouble to get at him, but I know his ways and caught him at last; he seemed very much interested."

"Really?" murmured Dreyel thoughtfully. "The question is whether he can help me now."

Murner smiled as if he had heard something funny.

"My dear Dreyel, you may rest assured that Maurice Wallion can help you. Don't you know that every one calls him the 'problem solver'? Why, man, it was he who only last summer unravelled the mystery of the 'Copper House,' and he has only lately returned to Sweden after working a whole twelve-month for the English government."

Murner spoke with all the enthusiasm of youth, and his praise would greatly have delighted the popular detective reporter of the daily paper, could he have heard it. As both men entered the studio Murner continued: "The question seems rather to be whether he *will*; you are so unnaturally reticent, Dreyel, but you can talk openly to him. I have known you for nearly a year now, and not one word have you ever said about yourself. What is this infernal secret you are carrying about with you? And if you persist in your obstinate silence, what is the use of asking Maurice Wallion to come here?"

"When he does I shall speak fast enough. If all you say about your friend is true, he'll see that he has not come here for nothing. Oh, yes, I'll speak out," Dreyel added slowly, "if only it is not too late!"

Murner shrugged his shoulders.

"He'll be here in an hour's time at the latest," he said, "I can't understand your anxiety; the wire you got this morning cannot possibly do you any harm."

"No, the wire can't; it's what will come after," replied Dreyel, making an effort to speak calmly.

"I haven't even seen it yet," remarked Murner.

"Forgive me," said Dreyel, absently thrusting his hands into his pockets, "here it is."

The young man eagerly seized the telegram which read as follows:—

"Victor Dreyel, John Street, 30, Stockholm.

"Toroni has got to know the secret. Watch the wooden doll. Expect me this evening between 8 and 9. E.R."

Murner was puzzled, he read it through once more but failed to grasp its meaning.

"Despatched from Gothenburg this morning," he said; "but who are E.R. and Toroni?"

At the mention of Toroni's name Dreyel set his lips and snatched the paper from Murner.

"Toroni?" he repeated after a pause, "Toroni ... he was the thirteenth."

He clenched his hands and relapsed into silence, and for a few seconds neither spoke. Rain and wind dashed against the window and a few stray, faded leaves gleamed like gold on the wet panes illumined from within. Dreyel was deadly pale, and the next moment he said in a strained voice:

"Don't ask me any more questions now, you will hear all when Maurice Wallion arrives."

He stopped, lost in thought; Murner cast an inquiring look at him. On the careworn face of the aged recluse there lay an expression of stern resolve which inspired the young man with a feeling of respect and reverence, and prevented his breaking the silence.

Furtively he looked round the large, gloomy room and shivered. The studio was about thirty feet by twenty with a sloping roof of small, dusty panes of glass in lead-setting, painted grey; a protruding bit of wall showed that the studio had been made by pulling down the partition between the two attics. A screen covered with some white and grey material, a movable kind of balustrade, a couch, a looking-glass and, above all, a huge camera under a green cloth and a small table littered with all sorts of photographic paraphernalia formed the inventory of the front part. At the farther end stood a simple writing table, a stool and a bookcase on which were exposed numerous photographs, the lower shelf being filled with books, mostly of a technical character. Two upholstered chairs flanked the book-case; on the right were two doors leading into the dark-room and Dreyel's sleeping apartment. A row of electric lamps, minus shades, cast a weird light over the vast, melancholy chamber which resembled a room in some dismal museum.

Murner's eyes scanned the photographs on the upper shelf; almost unconsciously he strove to evolve some sort of connection between that shelf and the mysterious telegram. Suddenly he started ... yes, there among the photos, in the top row, stood the wooden doll mentioned in the telegram!

He bent forward that he might see it better, but at the same moment Dreyel, who had been standing behind him, so altered his position that his shadow crept along the wall like that of an unwieldy wounded beast, stooping over the shelf as though something there needed protection. Murner was seized with a feeling of inward discomfort and muttered to himself, "What in the world have I to do with this odd old fellow's existence?"

His connection with Dreyel began in a somewhat casual way. When he (Murner) installed himself on the fourth floor of No. 30, John Street, he felt at once considerable sympathy for his taciturn fellow-lodger on the floor above. He had approached Dreyel with regard to some photographs of certain old houses in the neighborhood required for illustrating an article in one of the local papers; that had been the beginning of their acquaintance, and Dreyel appeared to have taken a genuine liking to the young fellow, who was rather inclined to discuss his future plans with an older, much-travelled and experienced man.

The curious rumors afloat respecting Dreyel's past had, of course, reached Murner also, but he had made no attempt to pry into secrets, the existence of which his own common-sense led him to consider doubtful.

But one day early in June, Dreyel, in Murner's presence, received a parcel by post from America. This parcel was to lead to important results. Murner, in his surprise, had exclaimed, "Oh, I say, it seems your friends in the States haven't forgotten you!"

His astonishment had been even greater when Dreyel opened the parcel. It contained only a little wooden image about eight inches high, representing a man in a workman's sweater, broad-brimmed hat and jack-boots, the whole being carved in dark, polished wood. It was a doll or rather a statuette skilfully executed. The features were broad and hard and bore a peculiarly life-like impress of defiance and brute force. Dreyel's face had assumed an ashen hue, but he allowed Murner to examine the curious little figure without a word. When, however, the latter ventured to put a few searching questions, Dreyel curtly replied:

"We shall see, this is only the beginning," and would say no more on the subject.

It was this identical wooden object Murner had discovered on the shelf in the studio, and this evening it inspired him with unaccountable aversion. In its brown face, hardly bigger than a man's thumb-nail, there seemed to lurk a fixed, diabolical grin, giving it the appearance of some loathsome fetish.

"Watch the wooden doll," repeated Murner. "It is nonsensical; first a wooden doll, and then that telegram…. The vile thing! Take it away, I can't bear it."

"Don't you touch it," said Dreyel sharply.

Murner had already put out his hands for it but drew back, surprised at the tone of Dreyel's voice. They stood face to face.

"What do you mean?" asked Murner, "Are you afraid of it?"

"No," replied Dreyel, "but no one must lay a finger upon it … not yet."

He took up a position between the shelf and Murner. When he saw the expression of Murner's face, he indulged in a cynical smile. "You are so impatient," he said, "I can't tell you any more just now, but perhaps the visitor I am expecting will…." He stopped abruptly. "Go down to your diggings, Murner, and leave me to myself; when your detective friend does come, he will find a tangle, even in his opinion, worth unraveling."

Murner was about to answer, but Dreyel's determined attitude prevented him, and he turned obediently towards the door. Then he looked round once more and said:

"Wouldn't it be better if I stayed with you?"

"No," replied Dreyel, "it will be better that you should receive Maurice Wallion downstairs."

He shook the young man's hand and said good-bye. Then he almost pushed him into the passage and closed the door.

It was nearly half-past eight when Murner reached his own quarters, below those occupied by Dreyel. He hung up his wet coat and went into his workroom or study. He felt ill at ease as if he had been drawn into a strange, antagonistic circle against his will. Dreyel's curious behavior both irritated and worried him. What was it that had really happened? He could not prevent his thoughts from dwelling on the telegram which, undoubtedly, had some connection with the wooden doll. Who could "E.R." be, whom Dreyel was so anxious to receive alone that evening? Who was "Toroni," and what secret had he got to know?

Impatiently Murner threw himself into an armchair in order to clear his confused brain.

The wooden figure had arrived from America early in June, and today, August the first, that wire from Gothenburg. The old man had been pacing to and fro in the studio overhead all the morning. Then came his unexpected visit about two P.M., when he was pale, but calm. "Will you render me a service, Murner?" he said, "I can't quite explain, but I have had a wire which has put me into a damned hole. You know Maurice Wallion well, don't you?"

Murner nodded, much surprised.

"Well, I want his help," continued Dreyel, "it means more to me than I can say; for God's sake make Maurice Wallion come at once."

Struck by the painful earnestness of Dreyel's words, Murner promised to find the ever busy and unget-at-able "Journalist Detective" whom he knew well. After a search lasting several hours, Wallion was discovered at last and listened with keen interest to what Murner had to tell him, but he said only:

"Remember me to your friend and tell him I will call at nine o'clock."

Murner had almost expected a refusal. Could it be possible that Maurice Wallion, with only such slight data to go upon, had already come to some conclusion regarding this wretched affair? And why did Dreyel seek his help now? Naturally he had often talked about Maurice Wallion with Dreyel, but if any serious danger threatened Dreyel, would it not have seemed more practical to communicate with the police? Murner's sensible mind was, for the time being, rather irritated by Dreyel's mysterious ways. Taking a good whiff at his cigar he said to himself: "All this is quite childish; his recluse life has affected his brain."

He laid down his cigar and listened intently for footsteps overhead, but all was quiet. What might Dreyel be doing now? The whole house was so still and silent, it might have been tenantless and empty; only the rain beat against the windows. He tried once more to collect his thoughts and calmly recall what Dreyel had said and his own words, but he had to give up the attempt. The bare remembrance of the wooden doll and the telegram was revolting; the whole thing was so foolish....

Suddenly he heard sounds above; some one was walking across the studio; he recognized Dreyel's steps, but immediately after he heard some one go up who seemed to move much more quickly; judging from the sound the steps proceeded from the waiting-room as Dreyel's had done. Murner was startled. So there was a visitor up there? It must have been true then, and the telegram had not been an ill-timed joke; and Dreyel's words had not been the outcome of a diseased brain. Surely the stranger must be the redoubtable "E.R." The steps halted for a few seconds, then turned towards the studio and when they ceased altogether Murner fancied he heard a dull thud, as of a heavy trunk or sack being deposited on the floor. His curiosity waxed stronger; he waited impatiently, but nothing more was to be heard. He tried to picture the situation. Most likely Dreyel and the mysterious visitor had drawn their chairs up to the writing-table and were having a long, subdued conversation; about what? The wooden doll?

Murner thrust his hands into his pockets and paced up and down the room, feeling much perturbed. He looked at the clock; it was twenty minutes to nine; twenty more long, tedious minutes must elapse before Maurice Wallion would come. Wouldn't it be better for him to go upstairs at once? Why such profound silence up there? No footsteps ... no anything ... He felt his heart beat; a wave of icy cold seemed to emanate from the stillness above. All at once he realized that possibly he was the only friend Dreyel had, the only one to whom the old man could as a last resource turn with his prayer for help!

He hurried to the door; as he was about to open it a shrill scream broke the silence of the house, and a door banged a long way off.

CHAPTER 2

"DO NOT LET HER ESCAPE"

Thomas Murner tore open the door and rushed into the passage. Had he for a moment dreamed that this proceeding would land him in an adventure destined to influence all his life and send him to the other end of the world, he might have thought twice before dashing out in such a hurry; but Fate had already cast the die. From that moment or rather from a quarter to nine on August the first, 1918, Thomas Murner became the hero of many a wild and curious episode.

At this point it may be as well to give a sketch of this young man's person, character, and position in life.

Thomas Murner, at twenty-eight years of age, was in many ways as lonely as Victor Dreyel; both his parents were dead and other family ties were little more than a myth to him, but he differed from Dreyel in that he was a cheerful, sociable and energetic young man, with the normal aspirations and keen intelligence of youth, instead of a soured recluse. In possession of a fair competence inherited from his father, ambitious, and cherishing great plans as a fully qualified architect, the future loomed brightly before him. After a short and laborious apprenticeship in an architect's office, he was now cast upon his own resources; his position at this time might have been much better if he had not devoted so much work and time to a "bright idea"; for "bright ideas" emanating from the brains of aspiring young men do not always meet with due appreciation.

Murner's "bright idea" had been the erection of a "Terrace House," but what sort of an edifice this was meant to be no one had had the patience or curiosity to inquire.

In person he was of medium height, thin, agile, with an impulsive manner, dark hair, blue eyes and an engaging expression of youthful self-reliance played round his mouth. Every one liked him, and liked him too well to take his "bright ideas" seriously, which amused more than it vexed him. Though skeptical he was ever hopeful, and was prepared to spend a few more years in attaining the realization of his dream, which took the form of a luxurious and prosperous office whence the "fashionable, famous architect" would issue orders and plans for the building of innumerable "Terrace Houses," but, as has been already observed, no one can foretell the future.

The first thing Murner heard when he stepped out of the half-dark roomy passage was the sound of some one coming out on the upper landing and shouting down the stairs: "Don't let her escape!" He recognized the croaking voice of the porter's wife, and cried: "What on earth is up?"

"Is that Mr. Murner? For God's sake come up here, something awful has happened ... but don't let that little monster escape."

The voice could be heard all over the house and, finally ended in an hysterical scream; every door was opened and people were heard coming up from the lower rooms. In two strides Murner was at the top of the stairs where he found the porter's wife, white with fear and shaking from head to foot, standing at the studio door.

"Quick, tell me what has occurred and who it is that must not be allowed to escape?"

"The girl in the grey dress," stammered the woman, "she came out of here."

"Out of the studio? Well, and what then?"

"She murdered Mr. Dreyel."

For a second Tom stood as if paralyzed, but the next moment he dashed through the waiting-room into the studio. On the floor right in front of the bookshelf lay Dreyel, face downward, his shoulders convulsively drawn up, his head and the upper part of the body turned on one side and both arms stretched out. Murner sank on his knees and put out his hands to turn the dead man over, but quickly drew back. Victor Dreyel was past human aid; a knife had penetrated through his clothes between the shoulder blades; his coat had been considerably crumpled by the fall.

The porter's wife suddenly burst into loud and uncontrollable weeping, but the young man strove to keep cool. From the woman's disconnected account he gathered that she was on her usual round, locking the doors, and extinguishing the lights; finding the studio door ajar she had gone in; struck by the unusual quiet she had proceeded to the other end, and, to her indescribable horror had found Dreyel lying dead on the floor.

"Well now, about the girl?" asked Murner impatiently, "the girl in grey?"

"She stood hidden behind that screen there, and when I screamed and was about to run away, she ran out of the door just in front of me and slammed it after her."

"What was she like?"

"I could only see that she was in grey; she fled past me like a cat and when I got to the door she was gone. I understood then that she must have killed him."

Murner interrupted her. "Telephone at once to the police," he said, "I shall remain here."

As she obediently went to the door he called after her, "You wait below for the police and make them send for a doctor."

Left alone he gazed for a few minutes at the still and lifeless object before him with dry and smarting eyes, for the tragedy unnerved him; it was so difficult to think that poor shrunken form in his threadbare clothes was a dead man; he knew that the dull thud he had heard while in his workroom, must have been caused by Dreyel's fall, and the light footsteps must have been those of the girl. Dreyel had never mentioned any girl to him....

He endeavored to collect his thoughts, and as he pondered on what Dreyel had or had not said, cursed the indifference with which he had listened to words, some of which, no doubt, had been of serious import. If only he had remained up there with him; it seemed almost as if he had betrayed the old recluse to his enemies.

Mechanically he went up to the writing-table where his attention was attracted by a white paper half concealed under the blotter; it was probably a half-finished letter. He began to read it, but the words failed to convey any meaning to his brain, and he caught himself staring again at the motionless body, when a sudden noise made him start violently. Had the police come already?

Unconsciously he stuffed the letter into his pocket and strained his ears to listen. Steps were audible in the waiting-room; yes, it was the police. Murner gave vent to a sigh of intense relief. Three detectives entered hastily, followed by the porter's wife. The chief detective was a pleasant, thick set individual, with a small, grizzled mustache; he looked round and, stopping short at sight of the corpse, said in a commanding tone, "Yes, things do look pretty bad up here. Has any one touched him?"

The porter's wife denied having done so, and he advanced a step nearer to the body. He cast a quick, penetrating look at Murner and said sternly, "Mr. Murner, I presume?" The young man bowed slightly. "I am Superintendent Aspeland. If I have been rightly informed you also live in this house and were intimately acquainted with the murdered man. Is that so?"

"I was acquainted with him, but not intimately."

"You were not present at the murder?"

"Certainly not," replied Murner, and he would have said more had not the superintendent prevented him.

"A young girl, dark, slender, very pale and dressed in grey is said to have run out of the house ... Did you see her? No? Do you know who she is?"

"No, I never heard of her before this evening," said Murner, wondering whether in this connection he ought to mention the telegram or his having heard strange footsteps. As though answering his unspoken thoughts the superintendent continued:

"I shall presently have a few more questions to put to you, Mr. Murner; perhaps you will be good enough to retire to your own quarters meanwhile. After what this woman has said it seems the girl never left the house at all."

"I can swear to that," broke in the porter's wife, "When she ran out of the studio, there were at least five or six people about or on the stairs, but not one of them saw her. She must have hidden somewhere, though I can't make out..."

"So much the worse for her if she *is* here," said the superintendent gruffly, "I have two men stationed in the yard and two more in the road; now I am just going to have a look round till the doctor comes."

He took out a pocket-book and pencil, beckoned to one of the other detectives, and bent down over the body. Murner profited by the occasion and left the landing, grateful for the relief; he longed for undisturbed solitude in which to think over recent events. Outside he encountered a dozen inquisitive tenants, mostly women, and beat a precipitate retreat from their alarmed inquiries. He found his door shut but not locked, though he remembered leaving it ajar in his hurry to go up to the studio, and supposed that some passer-by had closed it. He went in, locked the door and switched on the light. Catching sight of himself in the glass, he noticed that he was deadly pale, and seeing his own drawn, distorted features, he was seized with the most unreasonable fury against the inhuman wretch who had murdered Dreyel. "It is horrible," he said, to himself, "there is no possible excuse for such an act of brutality."

He took a draught of water and opened the door leading to his study, but remained on the threshold petrified ... some one was sitting in his armchair by the table!

It was the tall, slight figure of a girl in a simple grey costume and black silk hat! The large, half open brown eyes were set in a colorless, thin face; her lips quivered and her hands were tightly clasped over a leather satchel on her knee.

Their eyes met.

CHAPTER 3

THE GIRL IN GREY

Tom Murner closed the inner door mechanically from force of habit and leant against it. He began to wonder if he were dreaming. The girl sat still, immovable, but followed every movement of his with her eyes.

All of a sudden she said something but in so low a tone that he could not hear her words.

"What was it you said?" he asked hoarsely.

She continued staring at him with the same unnatural look in her eyes; but presently the bag slipped from her knees and he noticed that her hands were twitching convulsively. He was beside himself at the awkwardness of the situation and angrily inquired:

"How did you get here? Who are you?"

She rose from, her chair and said in a listless tone: "I *had* to hide, I want to get out of here."

She bent down to pick up her bag and burst into tears, then leaving the satchel on the floor, she made wildly for the door, but as Tom did not move she stopped short in front of him with bowed head, her whole form shaking.

"Let me go," she said. "Oh, God, let me get away from here!"

"The house is full of police," he answered deliberately. "They declare that Victor Dreyel met with his death at the hands of a girl in grey."

She staggered as though she had been struck. She moaned pitifully, lifted her hands to her throat and fixed her eyes upon his face as if dazed. The silent appeal in her feverishly burning eyes made him regret his harshness.

"It is not true," she said, closed her eyes and fell back in a dead faint. He caught her in his arms and carried her to the easy chair; her white blouse showed through the open grey coat. A wave of compassion surged through his brain as he saw how frail and helpless she was; small, pearly teeth gleamed between her half-open lips. She breathed faintly and her deathly pallor accentuated the thinness of her face; her expression was one of childhood innocence. For a moment he touched her hand, which was soft and warm. Could it be that these small hands were stained with the lifeblood of Victor Dreyel? He shuddered at the bare thought and yet how could the situation be explained? Here he was in his own room alone with a girl ... an entire stranger to him ... wanted by the police ... in a dead faint. He was at his wits' end.

"This can't go on," he reflected. "What on earth am I to do?"

She had not entirely lost consciousness, and he saw that her dark eyes were fixed upon his with a puzzled expression. Presently in a broken voice she said:

"I was hiding behind your door when you opened it; I heard people about and ran in here."

"You ran in here? And what for, may I ask?" he queried in despair.

"I did not want to fall into the hands of the police...."

"Then you must have some reason for being afraid of them?"

She looked down without answering; after a few seconds she glanced up again and asked, "Is there any one about who could hear me?"

The unexpected question startled him; he was about to reply in the negative, but his suspicious were roused, and he made a hasty examination of his rooms.

His quarters comprised three rooms—his study littered with sketches, plans and models; his living—or as he preferred to call it his smoke-room, with comfortable leather chairs; and his bedroom. At first he had intended to make his household a model one, but his various housekeepers having proved failures he had turned his domestic offices into lumber rooms. Returning from his investigation he said:

"There is no one about, and now, I trust, you will explain how you came to be found in the studio?"

"And supposing I can't?" she whispered.

"In that case I am afraid the police will make you!"

At that moment there was a violent ring at the outer door and Tom caught the buzz of voices. The ringing was renewed from time to time, accompanied by loud knocking; and he went towards the hall—as in a dream.

The girl jumped up without a word and threw her arms round him in order to hold him back. Her tears broke out afresh, and her flaming eyes made her look like a little fury; but he pushed her away and said in a decisive tone:

"Look here, this won't do, I must open the door."

"No, no," she whimpered, "you must help me.... I can swear ... Oh, do help me!" She covered her face with her hands and he heard her murmur: "There is no one in the world who will help me."

He did not release his hold of her and the small figure seemed to dwindle in his grasp: without knowing how it happened he found her head resting on his shoulder.

"Well, well, try to be calm," he said austerely "I never said I should hand you over to the police, did I?"

"No, you did not," she replied gravely "you did not."

She sighed and dried her tears.

"Go into the next room and keep quiet," he said hurriedly.

The girl hesitated, but another furious ring scared her and the next minute she had disappeared. Tom stuffed her satchel under some papers, looked round once more and found a grey glove on the chair which he bundled into his pocket and went to open the door. Superintendent Aspeland walked in.

"So this is where you live," he grunted, looking about him. "Yes, you seem to have all you want here. Have you heard anything of the woman since you came down from the studio? Have you seen her? What about that window there, does that look into the street?"

Tom drew a long breath.

"Are you referring to the girl in grey, Inspector?"

"Yes, of course."

"I know nothing more about her," said the young man in a loud voice; "but that window over there does look into the street," he added.

"Hm!" said the superintendent, who had already thrown open the window, and was looking up and down the road. He closed it rather noisily.

"I see," he mumbled, tugging at his mustache, "and what about that door over there?"

"Goes into the next room," Tom said, inwardly quaking. "It is..."

"Oh," remarked Aspeland carelessly, taking out pocket-book and pencil. "Oh, I say, I just picked up a telegram here."

He made Tom tell him what he knew about the telegram from Gothenburg, then he said rather crossly, "It seems to me as if no one here were capable of giving any explanation of this tiresome business! Oh, well, I haven't done with it yet; we shall see."

He stood still for a while without appearing to be looking at anything in particular, then he slowly walked out, shutting the door after him. Tom began to feel dizzy and to wonder what he really had been doing; had he really in cold blood been trying to bamboozle a police superintendent?

The door of the next room was gently opened and the girl came out. They looked at one another in silence. Tom essayed to speak, but his voice failed him. In his mind's eye he still beheld the lifeless body, and his wrath and indignation against the murderer broke out afresh.

"Anyhow, you were there," he said, hardness and suspicion in his tone.

The girl hung her head.

"Then you don't believe me?" she said in a low voice. "I ... I can't explain. It is so hard ... I am so awfully lonely."

Tom went a step nearer to her.

"If only you..." he began eagerly, then stopped abruptly. What had he been going to say? What did he know?

"Won't you tell me who you are?" he continued more gently. She shivered.

"No, I had better go; thanks for what you have done, and ... goodbye."

She put out her hand without raising her eyes, and let the small, soft fingers rest for a moment in his own. She withdrew them with a nervous exclamation. There was again a ring at the door as the church clock struck nine, and without uttering a word the girl ran back into the smoking room. "She trusts me," he thought, and he felt oddly touched, but quickly pulled himself together.

He went out into the hall, fully determined to tell the inspector everything. Was it not his duty? But when he opened the door he was completely taken aback; for without any ado, a tall, well set-up man in a mackintosh crossed the threshold, hung his hat on a peg and unbuttoned his coat.

"Good evening," he said in a deep, mellow voice, "this house seems more lively than I was led to believe. Where is your mysterious friend Dreyel?"

Tom stood as if turned to stone.

"Maurice Wallion, by Jove!" he said panting, "I had quite forgotten you were coming."

The journalist looked at him as he wiped the rain drops from his face. Tom felt like a guilty schoolboy before those calm grey eyes, and went hot all over. A sudden smile passed over the detective's usually grave and impassive features.

"I begin to suspect," he said, "that you ought to have called me in sooner. You promised me an interesting evening and the first persons I run into are two men from the police. What has happened? Has Victor Dreyel got himself into a mess?"

"He was murdered half-an-hour ago." said Tom.

Maurice Wallion bit his lip and cast a peculiarly keen look at the young man; then he slowly took his way to the study, looked round and said: "Too late, I see. Where and how did it happen?"

Tom, in an incoherent manner, told him. He mentioned his conversation with Dreyel at eight o'clock, the wooden doll, the telegram and the mysterious footsteps, finishing up with the suspicions of the police in regard to a certain young girl in grey.

But he went no further. Now, having recapitulated all the details in order, he himself for the first time got a clear insight as to how matters stood. A cold sweat came over him.

Up there, in the studio ... a dead man; down here in the very next room an unknown girl, possibly an adventuress, most likely Dreyel's murderess, in spite of her assertions to the contrary ... concealed in his own abode!

"I do believe you are turning pale," observed Wallion, who had been narrowly studying his friend's face; "got anything more to tell me?"

Tom hesitated.

"Wallion," he said at last, "do you believe the poor girl did it?"

"Who? Your girl in grey, the stranger? How should *I* know? Funnier things than that have happened."

Wallion looked annoyed and absent. He listened attentively to occasional footsteps overhead; without asking, he knew they came from Dreyel's studio.

"They have got something to think about now," he muttered with an odd flash in his eye. "I say, Murner, the story Dreyel might have told would have been worth hearing. Is that Aspeland walking about up there?"

"I think it must be," answered Tom feebly. He was in doubt as to what Wallion intended to do, and dared not ask; he kept thinking of the girl in hiding not ten feet away—thinking it might be better to let Wallion know that she was there. In his confusion he fancied that Wallion knew everything already, and was only making fun of him; he became desperate. He had the confession on the tip of his tongue. Better make a clean breast of it at once, he thought—and was just going to open his mouth when the journalist said: "If the wooden doll has disappeared, then the matter will be cleared up."

Tom drew a deep breath.

"What ... what do you mean?"

"Let us go up to the studio," was Wallion's answer: "if I judge the situation aright this is the most curious mystery I have ever had to deal with."

"*You* have had to deal with?"

"Yes, and I intend to get to the bottom of it too; I feel I owe it to poor old Dreyel."

He went out quickly. Tom followed, taking good care to shut the door tight this time. They went upstairs and into the studio.

Aspeland, two detectives and a well-dressed gentleman with a grey beard stood silent and transfixed in the middle of the room. All the lamps were lighted, and the Superintendent was busy making notes in his book.

"What do you want here?" he called out without turning round.

"Good evening, Aspeland," said Wallion, "how are you?"

Aspeland turned quickly.

"'The Problem Solver,' as sure as I am alive," he said awkwardly, "however did you get here? Are you a conjurer? Has the news of this tragedy already reached the town?"

"No, not the town, but it has reached me; it is something in my line of business you see. Have you got him fast?"

"Him? Who?"

"Why, the murderer, of course."

"Well it isn't a HE, it's a SHE," Aspeland answered, "and she is here in this house, and we are going to be after her."

"How do you know she is here in this house?"

"Because she was seen running out of the studio after the crime, also because nobody saw her go down the stairs, though heaps of people were about. I tell you she is in hiding somewhere not far off, and if I have to send fifty men after her I mean to catch her."

Wallion gazed thoughtfully at Tom.

"Oh, very well," was all he said. He thrust his hands into his pockets and took a good, long look round the studio. The body had been removed, but a dark red spot, scarcely dry, showed on the grey linoleum in front of the bookcase; it was but a small stain which could easily have been covered with an inverted teacup, but it was of supreme importance, and all eyes were automatically turned upon it, as Wallion bent over it. For several seconds there was no sound save the patter of the rain on the glass roof, and then Wallion inquired as to the whereabouts of the body.

"It has been taken into the bedroom," answered Aspeland. "The doctor says death must have been instantaneous, the man having been stabbed in the back," he pointed to the silent gentleman with the grey beard by way of introduction, and said, "Doctor Baum."

Having bowed to each other, the doctor laconically remarked, "A most cold-blooded murder—the work of an expert. Between the shoulder-blades—straight through the heart—internal hemorrhage, death practically instantaneous."

"Does the wound give any clue to the instrument used?"

"Yes, it must have been a sharp, long and narrow blade, possibly a daggerlike weapon, used with unerring precision."

Aspeland interrupted the doctor impatiently.

"Would you like to view the corpse?" he inquired of Wallion. "I am not against hearing your opinion," he added, somewhat clumsily, and called to one of the detectives: "Tell the porter's wife to come up again."

Then the superintendent, Wallion and the doctor proceeded to Dreyel's small, untidy bedroom. Tom followed in their wake, but he could not bring himself to go near the iron bedstead from which the doctor lifted the sheet.

"Let me look at his hands," said Wallion with decision, "and then help me to turn him over."

"The wound has closed, as you see," said the doctor, as if he were giving a lecture on anatomy, "an uncommonly well-directed blow—not a bone touched—the inquest will show..."

Tom shuddered and went back into the studio, the other three soon followed, and the doctor took up his hat.

"We shall meet again tomorrow," he said to Aspeland. "Good evening, gentlemen."

Wallion's face assumed a new expression; he seemed to have been deeply impressed at sight of the dead man, and Tom inquired anxiously, "Found out anything?"

The journalist looked at him for a moment.

"Tom," he exclaimed suddenly, "I wonder whether any man has ever been murdered from a more incomprehensible motive than your poor friend. Whoever it was who did the deed he is the vilest monster I ever came across, unfit to be called a human being. Yes," he added abjectly, "Dreyel, in his extreme need, begged for my help—I know why now—and the help came too late..." The muscles of his face were working. "But whoever it was that killed Victor Dreyel, he shall not escape."

Before Tom's eyes there rose a vision of a girl hidden in the dark room and, quaking with fear and apprehension, he listened to the steps of the pursuers. At last he asked: "What are you going to do?"

"I am going to unravel the mystery, of course," replied Wallion, rather irritably.

He went up to the portrait shelf and said, "It seems absurd, and yet it is true, Tom, this is the place where the wooden doll stood, isn't it?"

The young man shivered. Wallion was pointing to the upper shelf and to his dismay, Tom perceived that the little wooden figure was indeed no longer there; but Wallion gave him no time to speak. Turning to the superintendent, he suddenly remarked:

"Well, Aspeland, and what is supposed to have been the motive?"

The officer who was just then deep in conversation with the porter's wife, replied with some irritation:

"The motive, sir? That will be a question to be answered later on. Once we've got hold of the perpetrator the motive will reveal itself fast enough."

Wallion smiled at Aspeland's display of temper. He knew that clever, conscientious official of old and could make a shrewd guess at what had put him out. It would have been an immense gratification to the old veteran to have laid hands on a reckless criminal, but to run down a poor girl who might have been driven to commit the crime, and was now probably hiding like some hunted animal, was not at all to his taste. Wallion cast an interrogative glance at Tom and said:

"Isn't it rather a waste of time to wait here any longer?"

"What do you mean?" said the inspector in a grumbling tone.

"Would it not be more to the point to search for the short, slim individual who climbed on to the roof through that window there?"

Nothing in Wallion's tone gave the slightest indication that he attached any importance to his question, but all eyes turned to him and the official became uncomfortably red.

"Eh! What? Window ... I ... what window?"

"That one over there," said Wallion pointing to the one furthest from the door.

"Oh, that one," said Aspeland drily, hurrying towards it. "I saw that, you need not teach me observation; Dreyel may have closed it himself."

Wallion called his attention to a chair which stood under said window, and had on its seat the mark of a wet shoe.

"If you measure that mark you'll find that it was made by a shoe two or three sizes shorter than Dreyel's. Besides the window can only have been opened a few minutes or there would be some drops of rain about here, and it is not—as you say—closed. It has only dropped—as can be seen by the unturned bolt. You will notice also that the intruder, probably to facilitate getting on to the roof, stood on the fore part of his feet or toes, as the impression on the seat shows."

Aspeland stroked his chin.

"Well, well," he said deprecatingly. "But about the girl, the murderess? Apparently she had an accomplice..."

Wallion's manner and speech had so far been those of a calm, critical observer; now, he was roused, and in an authoritative voice, he said, "Aspeland, it was not a girl who dealt that blow. Dismiss all thought of her from your mind for the present; you don't believe me, but I say it again, some *man* has escaped through that window on to the roof. I maintain that it was he who murdered Dreyel. Moreover here is his card!"

Wallion went back to the shelf and pointed to its surface where the dust lay thick, except for a small space of perhaps three inches, indicating that some object which had lain there for a long time had recently been removed.

"Good Heavens!" exclaimed the porter's wife who had just come up, wringing her hands, "the wooden image has gone."

"Yes, it has," answered Wallion, "but Mr. Murner can bear witness that it was there at 8:30 this evening; the marks in the dust are irrefutable.... They were made by a coat sleeve with two buttons, therefore, undoubtedly, that of a man. At a guess one would say the shelf must be about three and a half feet in height, and the marks in the dust lead to the conclusion that the man must have been short of stature and slight, otherwise he could not have wriggled through that small aperture in the corner."

"If it happens to have been that one," growled Aspeland.

"Of course, but why shouldn't it have been that one? There were no marks of dust on Dreyel's sleeve, so it wasn't he who removed the wooden doll, and there was no one else here."

"No, but the wooden figure—what was the story about it?" broke in Aspeland. "A wooden image?" he added fixing his eyes on Tom. "That must have been a most wonderful thing, what do you know about it?"

"Nothing more than that Dreyel received the figure from America early in July," said Tom, describing the packet as well as he could. "That's all, but it must certainly have been the object alluded to in the telegram."

"Telegram, telegram," muttered the superintendent, looking round distractedly. "So there is a wooden doll and a man who..." his bloodshot eyes turned to the window in the corner. "Johnson," he cried, "go out and whistle for one or two men to help you, and then go and examine the roof minutely." Addressing the porter's wife he said:

"Did you happen to see a short, agile man anywhere about the house this evening?"

She shook her head. Aspeland sniffed.

"Come along with me," he said roughly, "we'll ask some of the other tenants; some one must have noticed him, seeing he was made of flesh and blood," and, giving Wallion an angry look, he went out.

The other detectives remained to keep watch on the window. Murner and Wallion lighted a cigarette and went out arm-in-arm, "Let's go down to your digs," said Wallion.

CHAPTER 4

"HE FRIGHTENED ME"

Tom stopped aghast at his door with the key in his hand. It was again half-open.

"That's odd," he murmured, "it begins to be quite uncanny; I could have taken my oath that this time I shut the door and locked it, too."

Wallion pricked up his ears. "*This* time?" he said.

"Yes, when the porter's wife gave the alarm I forgot it and left it open, but now? It certainly is very odd."

Wallion became much interested; secretly he measured the distance between the door and the stairs leading to the studio; but he made no remark, and turning the handle of the hall door walked in.

Tom who had changed color, laid a detaining hand on his arm.

"Maurice," he panted, "just a minute, I've got something to tell you."

Wallion turned his head and fixed his penetrating grey eyes on Tom.

"Look here, Tom," he said calmly, "a little while ago you asked me whether I thought the girl in gray was guilty? You then heard me insist that it was a man who had killed Dreyel. Do you take me?"

The young man was dumbfounded. Wallion smiled, opened the door and went in; all was dark.

"Didn't you leave the light on?" Wallion asked, standing still.

Tom, completely unnerved, trembled.

"Certainly I did," he stammered, "Maurice ... there is..."

"Stop," whispered Wallion, "there is some one crouching behind the inner door."

He fumbled for the electric button and found it after a time; the flash revealed a figure, huddled up against the wall of the study door. It was the girl in gray ... she might have been asleep, her head sunk upon her breast and her arms clasped round her knees. Wallion closed the outer door and bent over the motionless figure.

Tom endeavored to raise her head, but it drooped helplessly to one side.

"She has fainted," said Wallion, "we must take her somewhere, ... but where?"

"Lay her on the couch in the smoke-room," suggested Tom.

They lifted her carefully and laid her on the couch. As Tom was gently slipping a cushion under her head, she opened her eyes. "He did frighten me so," she said in a feeble voice.

"Who frightened you?" asked Tom.

"In the hall," continued the girl, more feebly still. "I was afraid of being alone ... and I crept out ... then he came down the stairs behind me ... and ... he frightened me so."

"Who was it? What was he like?"

She made no answer. Wallion bent down and saw that her eyes were again closed. He took Tom by the arm and made him look at her left wrist. A slender thread of blood had come from under the sleeve of her coat, and drops were falling on the couch.

"He not only frightened her, the beast, he must have hurt her too! Lend me a hand and let us help her off with her jacket."

They tenderly raised the unconscious form and divested her of her outer garment. The left sleeve of her blouse was saturated with blood; Wallion rolled it up gently and said:

"A nasty wound, but not necessarily dangerous; she probably put up her arm to save herself. Go and get some water."

With a practised hand Wallion bandaged the girl's arm whilst Tom stood by on tenter-hooks. Having finished his work, Wallion gravely scanned the face of his patient, who was breathing calmly and regularly; then he drew Tom into the study.

"Now, be quick and tell me the meaning of this," he said.

Tom unburdened his oppressed conscience in a stream of words; the girl had concealed herself in his rooms for fear of being taken by the police, but she herself had protested she was innocent.

"In Heaven's name, what shall we do with her, Maurice?"

Wallion listened attentively and then said:

"Yes, my good friend, the situation is undoubtedly embarrassing; our little unknown guest must choose between two things. Either she must put herself into the hands of the police or she must pass the night in your bachelor apartments. Present day conventions most certainly demand that..."

"Conventions be hanged!" burst out Tom in despair; "We can't leave the poor thing to her fate like this."

"She requires care," said Wallion. "She can't be moved without attracting attention, but there is a certain law which refers to 'accessories' to a crime."

Tom paced wildly up and down and did not notice the gleam of quiet humor in the journalist's eyes.

"This must be a punishment for my sins—a nice predicament to be in, by Jove—what on earth am I to do?"

Wallion pushed him into his armchair.

"Try to be quiet," he said, "and listen to what I have to propose. The girl did not kill Dreyel; on the contrary, the real murderer made an attempt to kill her too. We can't tell what business she had in the studio, she might have come only to warn Dreyel; anyhow, she certainly had. nothing to do with the murderer, and it might be ... mark you ... I only say it *might* be that if we hand her over to the police her last plight would be worse than the first. She had better make her confession to us, then we shall know where we are."

Tom raised his eyes. "Then you think...?"

"The girl must remain here, there's nothing else to be done."

"Yes, but ... that ... that..."

"Is a clear case for Mrs. Toby," swiftly interrupted Wallion, as he reached out his hand for the telephone receiver.

"And who the deuce is Mrs. Toby?"

"Mrs. Toby happens to be my housekeeper, she is a regular good old soul and can adapt herself ... turn her hand to anything."

Tom heard him call for his own number, and after a while, the response came: "Hallo! It is Wallion ... No ... Want your help immediately. Take a taxi to 30, John Street, and come up to the fourth floor, the name on the door is Thomas Murner.... Yes ... now—at once ... No, some one has been taken ill ... Yes ... Thanks ... Good-bye."

He restored the receiver to its place and smiled.

"She is used to obeying queer orders," he said. "You wait here, whilst I just go out and see what the police are doing."

With that he disappeared. Somewhat easier in mind, Tom sat quiet for a while; he still had a feeling of moving in a weird, incomprehensible dream; and wondered how it was going to end? He rose and he peered through the door of the smoke-room, the girl still lay where they had put her. Her thin face was very white but peaceful; she had the look of a sleeping child, tired after play. Where had she sprung from? Who might she be?

He continued walking up and down in his study, when a noise in the street below disturbed his meditations. He threw open the window and looked out. The shifting clouds and the rain had turned this August night into a very autumnal one, but the lamps of two motors cast a glaring light across the pavement, and he saw two men coming out of the house bearing a coffin, which they deposited in the larger of the two motors; he understood that they were taking Dreyel's body away.

Soon afterwards Superintendent Aspeland came out, accompanied by Maurice Wallion; they exchanged a few parting words and shook hands; Aspeland got into the other motor. When the party had gone Wallion returned indoors.

A few minutes later, he entered the study, flung himself down on a chair and said in a tone of considerable annoyance: "Aspeland ought to have had more men with him."

"Why?"

"Dreyel's murderer has got away!"

"You don't say so? How did that happen?"

"The detectives found clear proof that a man *had* got through the window on to the roof, precisely as I said, but he was no longer there. It so happens that at the back there are two unoccupied attics; he broke a pane of glass in one of them and by that means landed in a passage on the fifth floor. He must have slipped out at the very moment the girl went to your door; perhaps he recognized her—who can tell? Anyhow he attacked and stabbed her. By the last flight of stairs he came upon the police, so without more ado, he rang the first bell he saw. When the door was opened he pushed the servant aside, ran through one of the rooms, opened a window looking into the street and jumped out—that's all. When the men started in pursuit he had disappeared in the darkness. Aspeland, meanwhile, saw I had been right and at once despatched men in all directions to catch the criminal, who really was—as I surmised—very short, spare and agile; he had on a green mackintosh and a felt bowler, but no one saw his face, and the 'mack' was subsequently found on a seat in the churchyard. For all the good that clue is, I don't envy the police."

Curiously enough the story of the assassin's escape seemed to afford Tom Murner a certain amount of relief; somehow it rendered his own position a trifle less compromising, and as the police were everywhere on the watch for the man, things looked decidedly better.

"Did Aspeland say anything more about the girl?" he asked.

"No. Aspeland is a clever fellow and has had experience, he is always ready to tackle a job, but will brook no interference. Just now he seems to have forgotten her."

"So much the better."

"Yes, but there are still detectives in the house, and I have seen among them, a sharp little chap called Ferlin, one of the cleverest spies in the force. The porter, too, is keeping his eyes open, and so from this time forward you must be officially on the 'sick-list.'"

"I ... on the 'sick-list.'"

"Exactly, and, indeed, you really don't look at all well since this tragedy occurred. We shall have to exaggerate things a little ... as an excuse for certain other matters; therefore, your nervous system has gone all wrong, so you have asked me to stay and keep you company for a few days ... and I have sent for my housekeeper to look after us both."

"I get you——!" said Tom.

"Well, isn't it true? The story is a little thin, I grant, but that can't be helped. How is the girl now?"

"I believe she is asleep."

"Good! Early tomorrow morning we'll send for a doctor I know, who won't say any more than is absolutely needful. And now, whilst we are waiting for Mrs. Toby, you might as well tell me—even to the minutest detail, what took place at the studio in the afternoon."

He lay back in his chair and listened attentively, now and then helping the younger man out by judicious questions. When he bad all the facts clearly before him, he quietly put on his considering cap.

"Dreyel, I suppose, obstinately kept to his secret to the last," he remarked. "He wanted help and yet received the mysterious 'E.R,' quite alone. The paradox is only on the surface ... it may be assumed that he himself was anxious for an explanation though he feared danger at the same time. To speak plainly, he anticipated news from 'E.R.' and danger from Toroni. It is impossible to ascertain whether Toroni himself was a personal danger or only the source from which it might spring. It can only be surmised that the man who has just escaped had some connection with Toroni the 13th. Again, I should not wonder if the girl on the couch might turn out to be 'E.R.'"

"I have had my suspicions all the time," said Tom, "but that would be awful ... awful."

"Awful? I don't see that, we know nothing about that. Everything considered, it is clear there exists some secret of supreme importance to Dreyel and one or two other persons in America. A certain man named Toroni had got to know the secret and it was in danger. Therefore 'E.R.' was sent to warn Dreyel; but when 'E.R.' arrived at the studio, Dreyel was found dead, slain by his adversary or his adversary's agent. To me that seems a natural conclusion."

"And the wooden doll?"

"I confess that is an extraordinary detail, though 'detail' is hardly the right word; the wooden doll is, so to say, the central figure in this mysterious problem; let us, therefore, follow its track. First, then, the doll was sent to Dreyel from America. Secondly, it worried him as though he expected something unpleasant to follow. Thirdly, in a telegram from 'E.R.' he was admonished to keep a watchful eye upon the doll since Toroni had learnt the secrets. Fourthly, before 'E.R.' could have a personal interview with Dreyel, he was murdered by some one who stole the wooden doll. One can't overlook the importance of the odd little figure. Tell me, did you ever have it in your hands?"

Tom nodded. "Yes, the very first time Dreyel showed it to me."

"Was it hollow inside?"

"No, it was absolutely solid wood throughout."

"Was there nothing to unscrew?"

"No, certainly not."

Rather disconcerted, Wallion said: "And wasn't there a mark of any kind?"

Tom sat up. "Well, now that you have mentioned it, I do recollect having noticed some figures cut in the wood on the sole of one of the feet."

"Aha!" exclaimed Wallion.

"Wait a minute, I've got it, I remember quite well what they looked like."

Tom drew a piece of paper towards him and proceeded to draw what was meant to represent the outline of the sole of a foot, in the middle of which he drew the following figures:

No. 12
33"

Wallion inspected this sketch with a frown and gave a low whistle. "So, ..." he said, "our materials are accumulating, but we are not much the wiser for all that....

"Did No. 12 apply to the wooden figure or was it meant to indicate that something was camouflaged as No. 12? Dreyel always spoke of Toroni as the thirteenth. That almost seems to tally, the wooden doll No. 12 and Toroni 13 ... but let us proceed warily with our theories for the present. Now what about the other figures? They may mean 33 inches or 33 minutes, or they may belong to some private code."

As Tom was about to make some impetuous remark, Wallion raised a deprecating hand, saying:

"Beware of obstacles, Tom; if we begin with mere suppositions we shall soon run our heads against a wall, perhaps we had better let the girl tell her story first."

Just then a car drew up at the door. Wallion listened and rose from his chair.

"Auxiliary troops, Tom," he said, smiling ... "Mrs. Toby to the fore."

He went out, and a few minutes later reappeared with a stout, elderly woman, dressed in black, with white hair; her still, comely countenance and regular features bore a stamp of strength and quiet content.

"I quite understand," she said to Wallion, who had probably already given her instructions. "I'll do what I can." Her kindly eyes rested upon Tom, and she curtsied; that was all the introduction. Then they all went into the smoke-room.

The girl had not stirred. Wallion pointed towards the white figure and said: "There's your patient, Mrs. Toby."

The old dame was already bending over the couch, and her deft fingers at once rearranged the cushion and the girl's clothes, which had got untidy. In a gentle, motherly way she crooned over her: "Such a poor little bird! Would any one believe that two big, stupid men hadn't even the sense to relieve her of her hat!"

The two men, like awkward schoolboys, stood and heard her remarks in silence; she removed the girl's small hat and handed it to Tom. "Now then, go and hang it up," she said, seeing the young man standing irresolute with his hands full. Having examined the bandage and felt the girl's pulse, she said: "The child is feverish. Please bring in my luggage, Mr. Wallion, and you, Mr. Murner, make haste and put a saucepanful of water on the gas-stove to boil."

She looked round and went into the bedroom, where she at once made herself at home. She took clean sheets out of a cupboard, and at one fell swoop turned out Murner's dressing-gown, slippers, smoking-jacket and shaving tools—in fact all his personal belongings—which she deposited in the smoke-room.

"I ought really to turn you out also, but I'll let you stay," she said, laughing, but hustling him out of the apartment. "I am mistress here now."

Tom ventured to say: "Can't I help you?"

"Rubbish!" answered Mrs. Toby, as she lifted the girl from the couch and carried her into the bedroom, shutting the door after her.

Wallion had settled himself comfortably in the study, and with an amused smile he said to Tom: "Mind you don't get in Mrs. Toby's way, she was born to rule."

They had a good smoke, and could hear at intervals sounds of Mrs. Toby's industry and energy.

"There's one thing that perplexes me," presently said Wallion, "to judge from appearances the girl must have come up from Gothenburg by the morning train; but people don't generally travel without luggage or with empty hands."

Tom smote his forehead with his hand.

"Good Heavens!" he cried, "her satchel!" he drew the black satchel from the papers under which he had concealed it.

Wallion nodded approval, and said complacently:

"That may help to clear up a lot."

The little bag had only the ordinary fastening; seeing Tom hesitate, Wallion took it from him and forthwith emptied the contents on the table. A lace handkerchief, a small silver purse containing Swedish money, various "vanity" articles, and lastly a hundred-dollar note, nothing more.

"Is that all?" asked Tom, when Wallion had finished; but with a curiously absent manner the journalist once more examined the satchel.

"No, that is not all," he said at last, hurriedly taking out another object and setting it on the table, "there is that."

"The wooden doll," ejaculated Tom, and a cold wave seemed to pass over him; vague but horrible thoughts floated through his brain. He saw before him a figure carved in hard, brown wood, eight inches high, representing a man in slouch hat, sweater, cartridge belt and high lace-up boots; but on more minute inspection he breathed a sigh of relief, the little figure bore a distinct resemblance to the one which had stood on Dreyel's shelf, but it was not the same.

"This is another," he said, taking it up; "but I say, I do believe ... it is an exact likeness of Victor Dreyel."

This discovery completed his consternation; the brown face was an exact representation of the murdered man, to his most characteristic and peculiar features. He looked at the sole of the doll's feet and there found an incised mark, No. 5 ... Nothing more.

"Look here," he said, "this one also bears a number."

Wallion took and silently examined it, whilst Tom's whole body quivered with excitement.

"What do you think it means?" he asked eagerly. "This is the third time we have come up against a number; it is very odd, but on the other doll there was in addition the number '33' ... Why not the same on this one? What do you make of it?"

Wallion said nothing, but his eyes grew bright; he smiled, took out and lighted a cigar; then he once more searched every corner of the satchel with renewed interest, till he came upon a pocket in the lining, whence he extracted a small note-book bound in leather. It contained only a few leaves, on the first of which the friends noticed two addresses, written in small, dainty characters: Victor Dreyel, 30, John Street, Stockholm ... and Christian Dreyel, Captain Street, Borne. There was nothing else written in the book, but four or five visiting cards fell out, each one bearing the same name: "Elaine Robertson." The two men looked at one another.

Wallion said: "'E.R.'! At any rate the question of that name is settled now."

At this juncture Mrs. Toby, hot from her work, came in with the tea-tray. "There," she said in a motherly tone, "I thought you gentlemen might be glad of a little refreshment; the young lady is asleep, but the fever seems inclined to be obstinate; she has been talking a rare lot of nonsense about a doll, and what it's all about I'm sure I don't know, but she never said what her name was."

"Her name is Elaine Robertson," replied Wallion, "and early in the morning I shall call in a doctor."

CHAPTER 5

THE OTHER DREYEL

When Mrs. Toby had left the room Wallion said: "Did you know that there were two men named Dreyel?"

Tom shook his head.

"I never heard Christian Dreyel mentioned, maybe he is a brother. I don't know."

The young man's voice sounded listless and tired; the existing complication seemed too much for him, his brain was in a whirl; he only longed to get away from it all and go to sleep. With a prolonged yawn, thrusting his hands into his pockets, he said:

"Perhaps we had better send a telegram to the other Dreyel; he is, naturally, the person most nearly concerned…. Hallo! what's this?" He broke off suddenly and from his pocket he drew forth a gray glove and a crumpled piece of paper.

"Look here, Wallion, here's a letter I found on Dreyel's table."

Wallion took the letter and began to read it, lifting his eyebrows. "This is prime stuff, of the first order," he said, "a letter from Victor Dreyel to Christian Dreyel…."

He read the epistle out loud: "Dear Christian," it began. "You are quite right, miracles do not happen now-a-days but justice may prevail in the end. The wooden dolls were only the beginning, a caution, a warning. Today I got a telegram which I enclose. Who is it from? I don't know whether it is true that Toroni is still alive, but if he is, strange things are likely to happen. They are all gone ... all, that crazy Craig Russel, Sanderson, the black Colonel, all gone. All, save William Robertson, myself and you, and the mystery of King Solomon is not solved. Fifteen years have I been living in this somber and quiet corner; perhaps it was my time of probation all along. They say likenesses of the dead bring misfortune to the living. After all those years it was a curious gift to you and me; and whatever may happen tonight, I shall not give in without a struggle..."

Wallion stopped. "It is not finished," he said, "Death stepped in between."

"King Solomon's secret," repeated Tom. "Secret indeed ... What a loathsome word! And what has Elaine Robertson to do with King Solomon's affairs?"

Wallion looked at the wooden doll and said:

"Your inquiry is premature ... we are still in the dark. The secret has acquired a name, that is all ... King Solomon; and King Solomon may stand for a place, a nickname, or for anything you like. You should rather ask what connection there can be between 'E.R.' and William Robertson? Well, to begin with both are alive at present, whereas another lot of persons, who evidently also had something to do with King Solomon are dead; among the latter are 'that crazy Craig Russel, Sanderson and the black Colonel,' and several others, whatever sort of folk they may have been. These, as well as Robertson and the two Dreyels, were in the secret for more than fifteen years, until a third party, by the name of Toroni, stepped in and discovered it, which threatened evil consequences. Toroni's informants were known and the bare mention of his name was enough to terrify Victor Dreyel: in short, Toroni was the villain of the piece. Again, only William Robertson and the two Dreyels being alive, it is plain that 'E.R.' must have been sent by Robertson to warn the others; the wooden dolls also ... mystic emblems ... must have come from Robertson! Must, did I say? We are pursuing wild conjectures, and here am I sitting and only making rough guesses."

"But you are right," said Tom, struck by Wallion's words. "It must be as you say, you have already brought the problem within measurable distance..."

"Have I?" said Wallion, laughing. "Yes, I have confined it to the obscurity of fifteen years, and located it in the continent of America ... a child might have done that much. No, no, my lad, it won't do to make any deductions from those infernal wooden dolls. They are irrational objects and before we get at the reason of their existence we may have to cast our present theories to the winds."

"Yes, but I suppose you have formed some point of view..."

"Three points of view, my friend. First, that this is the most glorious problem it has ever been my luck to handle. Secondly, that I can't understand it at all. And thirdly, that I want to go to sleep now."

He drew up a chair, stretched his legs upon it, leant his head against the back and was fast asleep in a few minutes. The rain continued to come down in torrents, flooding the gutters. The clock struck eleven. Battalions of wooden dolls marched past and cast evil glances at Tom. Their small, polished, sphinxlike faces glowed in the darkness like live sparks and voices from thousands of throats came through the shadows, crying: "We are the riddle, the mystery of King Solomon is ours." ... Then he seemed to hear sounds of weeping and felt a warm, soft little hand in his. "It is not true," he heard a girl whisper.... "I have killed no one, but I am so lonely ... no one will help me ..." Tom was just going to reply, but Elaine fled away through black clouds, and then he heard stealthy footsteps ...

Tom Murner jumped up confused and benumbed with cold. He had spent the night on the hard couch in his study, and the recollection of his horrible nightmare affected his nerves. In a moment everything which had occurred since yesterday afternoon unrolled itself like a film before his mind's eye; he put his hands up to his aching head and shivered with apprehension. Victor Dreyel's dreadful end, the girl hidden in his bedroom, the fiendish wooden doll still standing on his writing-table, everything passed before his mental vision. He looked round and stared at the designs for his "Terrace" houses as if he had never seen them before; something was different, but it was nothing tangible or outside ... the change was within his own soul. From a world of books and dreams he had all at once been flung into a life of adventure. Fate had decided and the great comedy which is enacted but once in a lifetime had begun. A small, pleading voice whispered in his brain: "Nonsense, such a thing could not happen. She may be innocent or she may not. See that she gets away from here as soon as possible, and see that you have nothing to do with her." The conflict in his mind began anew; he marvelled at the clearness with which he remembered every act, every word, yes, every gesture of hers. He jumped up and stretched his limbs. The ghostly monitor persisted: "Don't meddle with what you don't understand. Don't meddle with..." "Well, and what then?" he reflected, "is one ever justified in refusing to help another?"

He threw up the window and drew a deep breath, there were still clouds about, but the air was clear and fresh. Presently he heard the sound of voices proceeding from the smoke-room; Wallion and Mrs. Toby were talking and the name Elaine Robertson caught his ear. The journalist soon came out, walked into the study and closed the door after him; he looked very serious.

"I see you are awake, good!" he remarked drily; "There's much to be done. With Aspeland's assistance I have already gone through Dreyel's papers. Christian turns out to be a cousin of his; other relatives there are none; as for the rest of his papers there was nothing in them worth consideration."

Wallion then took up the wooden doll and put it in his pocket. "I am going to take that with me now, and for the present you mustn't say anything about it. The Chief Detective will probably call here, so mind you don't forget that you are on the sick-list. You are at liberty to say all you know, but nothing in any way relating to 'E.R.' Mrs. Toby has had her instructions."

"All right, but how is...?"

"The little lady? She is very feverish from her wound, but you need not be alarmed; the doctor will be here before long, ostensibly to see you ... hallo! Who's coming now...?"

There was a ring at the door and Superintendent Aspeland was admitted. He was accompanied by Detective Ferlin, and both men looked excited.

"Gone, without leaving the slightest trace behind him," Aspeland said, turning to Wallion. "Since the miscreant got out of the house he has disappeared from human ken like a 'U' boat."

"And is as great a danger," added Ferlin. "In my opinion that man is the greatest menace we have ever come across. But we must not forget the girl; she must have something to tell."

Detective Ferlin was short of stature, grave and alert, somewhat excitable and fidgetty, inclined to be a little bumptious, but clever and shrewd beyond the average. Aspeland tugged at his moustache and looked at his colleague sideways.

"Ferlin," he said, in an amicable tone, "I posted you and Rankel at the door, but both the assassin and the girl seem to have neglected to make your acquaintance. Have you any advice to give?"

Ferlin turned crimson to the roots of his hair, gazed for a moment at Tom and said: "Mr. Murner, will you give me an answer on one point?"

Tom grew as rigid as if ice were sliding down his spine, but he replied calmly: "Yes, of course, what is it you want to know?"

"Mr. Murner, you came out into the hall precisely at the moment the girl came rushing down the stairs. Did you not see her?"

"If you wish it I can affirm on oath that I never saw a shimmer of her," replied Tom, truthfully, and he could not refrain from laughing at something which only Wallion knew. Ferlin glowered at him with an ironic smile.

"Excuse me," continued Tom, "my laughing arose purely from nervousness ... You will understand."

"I understand," grunted the little man.

"This is no child's play, Mr. Murner, so you had better be careful.... The girl may be out of reach—we must just see. I, for one, shall keep my eyes open, though they mayn't be so fine as her own."

"By Jove! what a talker you are," remarked Aspeland. "Now, Mr. Wallion, Ferlin and I must have a little conversation about this Christian Dreyel, and be ready to answer a heap of questions when the Head of the Department arrives on the scene ... good-bye till then."

Ferlin and he went out together, and soon after sounds of people busy at work overhead became audible.

Wallion grew impatient and began to pace the room.

"What time is it?" he growled. "Half-past eight? Confound it all! Tom, before night I have to be at the other Dreyel's. I have no time for arguing. No, I don't want your company; it would only drag you deeper into the mire and I believe Ferlin is already thinking of arresting you...."

"What? Me...?"

"Yes, just you. We shall hear what the Chief Detective will have to say to the only intimate friend Dreyel had ... If they knew that the girl..."

He lifted both hands, and they exchanged glances.

"Wallion," resumed Tom in a low voice, "I have made up my mind, I mean to do all I can to help Miss Robertson, but I won't abuse your friendship if you are not inclined for a game of Hide and Seek with the police or the law."

Wallion's eyes sparkled—his expression was comical.

"You are talking like an idiot; who said anything about the law? And as to circumventing the police, I should soon put a stop to that. What are you making such a fuss about? Can't the girl remain quietly where she is?"

"Yes ... but..."

"No buts ... There's the doctor."

Wallion himself went to the door and a middle-aged man with a jovial, ruddy countenance walked in, and was introduced by Wallion as the "Doctor"—no name being mentioned. He seemed to be acquainted with the facts of the case, and with a formal bow to Tom, he came further into the room. Presently Mrs. Toby appeared at the door and beckoned to Wallion to come out ... Seeing Tom about to follow she shook her head. "I don't want a procession," she said crossly, and slammed the door.

Wallion went into the bedroom where he found the doctor standing by the window and writing a prescription. Without turning round the latter said: "Mr. Wallion, I shall keep a quiet tongue about what I have seen, but one thing I feel bound to tell you. The girl is a physical wreck. The wound is nothing. Make her take this now, Mrs. Toby, and again tonight, and by tomorrow the fever will be gone. What she wants is good nursing, and above all no excitement ... She has already gone through more than such a delicate constitution as hers can stand. She appears to have no means, and is half-starved and thoroughly worn out."

Wallion threw a hasty glance at Mrs. Toby who, accustomed to give her opinion, said without any preamble: "Starved she is not, but that she has not got any money is true. Her clothes are of the best stuff, and though threadbare, made by a first-class tailor. Her hands show no traces of hard work. She is undoubtedly a girl of good social standing. Last night when her mind was wandering, she kept calling for 'Father,' sometimes in English, sometimes in Swedish, poor little lamb."

"Did she say anything else?"

"Yes, she raved about dolls, and frequently mentioned the name of Toroni."

Wallion nodded his head and was soon lost in thought. He took a long look at the sleeping girl with her white face and little black curls. Her gentle, regular breathing pleased him particularly as seeming, more than anything else, to prove her feeling of perfect confidence in her strange surroundings, and as he looked at her more closely he noticed the look of almost child-like peace on her wan, refined features. It struck him the more when he remembered how he had last seen her with eyes wide open, a prey to the world's cruelty and wickedness. He turned away sadly.

"I have a great mind to try an experiment, Doctor," he said, "if you will give me leave."

"As long as you don't frighten her," he answered, coming nearer to the couch. "She still has a temperature, and her mind wanders at times."

Wallion bent over the sleeper. Half aloud he uttered the name "Toroni"; her breath came a little faster and she frowned slightly. He repeated the name once more. In a clear, child-like voice she said: "Yes, oh yes ... No. 13 Toroni ... Number six and number twelve ... Take care ... They are coming ... Father ... Papa, papa..."

Wallion straightened himself and looked at the doctor. His eyes betrayed an inclination to laugh though he was sorely perplexed; after a while he said: "Do you think she is wandering now, doctor?"

The doctor shook his head. "No, she is not wandering now, she is talking in her sleep."

"Dreaming?"

"No, the name you mentioned awoke subconscious memories and pictures." The doctor took Wallion by the arm and led him into the study.

"Leave her in peace now," he said. "Mrs. Toby is an excellent nurse, and unless anything particular happens I need not call again. Good-by."

Tom heaped question after question upon Wallion who recounted what had taken place. "She is all right," he added feelingly, "all right, Tom, I would take off my hat to any girl without friends and without means who could take such a load upon her shoulders."

Tom shook his friend's hand warmly.

"There are cases in which it is expedient to trust a little in one's intuition," continued Wallion thoughtfully, "at least until one has made all due investigations ... Have you a timetable handy? Thanks. Where is Borne? Oh, Borne seems to be one of the stations north of Gävle. Now listen, Tom, if Victor Dreyel had in his possession a wooden doll which it was worth while committing murder for, might not Christian Dreyel be in possession of one like it? May he not also have one of those 'likenesses' of the 'dead' which bring misfortune to the 'living'? Do you remember the unfinished letter and that the unseen culprit is still at liberty. Well, I intend to go to Borne, or perhaps..."

Again there was a ring at the door.

"Your doorbell has started business," grumbled the impatient Wallion, as he went out into the hall.

"Next man, please," he said. It turned out to be Aspeland.

"The Chief isn't coming," he said. "He is busy sending out scouts after the assassin and the young lady that porter saw—only in his dreams, I do believe—so you won't be bothered any more. I'm off now, but if anything happens Ferlin will be close at hand."

He went and Wallion whistled softly to himself.

"It rather seems as if they had their hands full," he remarked. "So much the better, it gives us another day's breathing time. You keep mum here, obey Mrs. Toby, and don't think too much about the little girl. Now, I am going to look after some affairs of my own in case the business in hand should drag on much longer, then I shall go up to Borne. Au revoir, we shall meet tomorrow."

* * * *

It was already dusk when the "Problem Solver" arrived at Borne.

Some Gävle newspaper reporters who had spotted him in the train, had made interesting attempts to discover the object of his journey, but Maurice Wallion was not inclined for company. All his thoughts were concentrated upon the mystery of the wooden dolls, on the foolish yet tragic row of wooden images which seemed one by one to peer at him through the darkness. One of them had found its way over Victor Dreyel's body into the pocket of the vanished enemy, another he had in his own ... would a third be found at Christian Dreyel's? If so, might not the assassin, too, be on his way there? Step by step he had been through every compartment of the train without finding any one whom it would be worth while suspecting. Maurice Wallion was decidedly growing uneasy, a most unusual and unaccountable proceeding on his part. He felt that he had not got a sure or firm grasp of the case. Was another catastrophe about to happen? ... Was he again coming too late? With quick steps he walked through the little village; he had been told at the station that Captain Street was half-an-hour's walk from there, but he stepped out so briskly that twenty minutes found him at the door of a low, lonely, dilapidated building, which answered to the description given him. He opened, or rather lifted the rickety gate and ran up through the garden, which was overgrown with rank grass, among gnarled fruit trees. A couple of rooks, croaking dismally, flew down from the roof, but there was no one to be seen. Wallion knocked loudly at the door.

CHAPTER 6

THE TRACK OF THE "INVISIBLE" ONE

After waiting a few minutes, Wallion heard footsteps approaching and the door opened. A tall man with a stoop, of coarse, ungainly build, about fifty years of age, stood before him. The individual in question had long, thick dark hair and an unkempt beard, but there was an indisputable resemblance to Victor Dreyel. Wallion raised his hat and said: "Mr. Christian Dreyel, I presume?" The man looked at him with undisguised curiosity.

"My name is Wallion and I am the bearer of a letter from your cousin."

"The door was open," he said in a deep bass voice. "You need not have knocked. Come in, Mr. Wallion."

"With your leave," said Wallion, "but I thought doors were meant to be shut." With which sarcastic remark he closed it after him.

Dreyel frowned and said: "Where is the letter?"

They entered a simple but comfortably furnished room, lighted by the dazzling golden rays of the setting sun.

Wallion took the letter Murner had found on the dead man's table from his pocket and silently handed it to Christian Dreyel. The latter stopped in the middle of reading it and observed: "He says he was enclosing a telegram. Where is it?"

"I can repeat it to you from memory," said Wallion evasively, at the same time doing so. The man nodded and continued to read.

"The letter isn't finished," he said, and his face began to twitch nervously with evident emotion.

"Tell me everything, quick, I am not nervous. What have you come here for?"

"Then you have not read the papers nor heard any news from Stockholm?"

"No."

"It is ill news that I bring, Mr. Dreyel. Your cousin was murdered in his studio last night by an unknown individual who has escaped. He left no papers, except this letter, which could throw light upon the tragedy. The telegram mentioned is in the hands of the police."

Christian Dreyel had gone to the window, through which he gazed in silence. A long pause ensued; at last he said:

"Are you from the police, Mr. Wallion, or not?"

"No," replied the journalist, "I came here to show you this," taking the wooden doll from his pocket and placing it on the table.

Christian turned in his chair, crossed his arms and examined the small wooden image without touching it or uttering a word. After a time he remarked: "Where did you get that?"

Wallion answered: "Allow me a question first. Do you happen to know 'E.R.'?"

At the mention of the initials Christian Dreyel made a movement of surprise, leant forward and said; "'E.R.' a woman ... what age?"

"About twenty."

"I don't understand," murmured Christian Dreyel, sinking back in his chair. "Only twenty, you say ... then she can't ... Elaine? What has she to do with the wooden dolls?"

"I got that doll from her. You see it has the features of your cousin Victor Dreyel and Elaine Robertson was in the studio at the time of his death."

"And the other one which was my cousin's own property?"

"The assassin stole that."

Christian Dreyel bent his head. Nothing seemed to surprise him. Wallion looked into the man's deep-set eyes. They were burning and Wallion guessed that Christian Dreyel was making a supreme effort not to exhibit an atom of feeling before a stranger. But as Wallion did not open his mouth, he said in the same calm tone as before: "Won't you tell me ... all?"

Darkness was gathering in the corners of the room and the golden light of the western sun had resolved itself into a narrow glowing band. Wallion began his story and Christian Dreyel listened in silence. When it was finished the two men could no longer distinguish each other's faces; the sky was covered with clouds of a bluish gray, the woods rose black and grim round Captain Street, and all was as silent as the desert. When at last Christian Dreyel spoke, Wallion was startled; he could scarcely recognize the voice.

"You seem to attach great importance to the wooden dolls, Mr. Wallion," he said in a hoarse tone.

"I do," answered Wallion; "and I believe the reason is pretty evident, 'likeness' of the 'dead' bring misfortune upon the 'living' ..."

Christian got up to light an oil lamp, and Wallion saw how the man's hand shook. He put the lamp on the table and gazed vacantly into space. His face looked ten years older but it had lost some of its hardness, and his emotion evidently overpowered him for he said gently:

"Thank you for coming. My poor cousin and I had not much in common, but he was my only relative. And now..." he broke off ... "you want to hear the truth, I know. Honestly, and without any ulterior motive: I would say to you, have nothing to do with the King Solomon mystery; let it be. It is hopeless to dig up the past, and evil often follows."

"My good Dreyel, it seems to me the digging process has begun already ... you forget No. 13 Toroni."

A curious expression came into Dreyel's eyes.

"With all your cleverness, sir, I believe you underrate the extent of the mystery," he replied. "Toroni, well, he really was the thirteenth, but I am not superstitious. Toroni has been dead more than fifteen years."

"Dead, you say? That is not possible; the telegram sent by Elaine Robertson distinctly says that Toroni has got to know the secret."

"Who is Elaine Robertson?" inquired Dreyel. "She may be William Robertson's daughter, what of it? What is her object? Perhaps you think I know everything," he went on, "yet you must have noticed how little my cousin knew—how he worried himself with vague presentiments and uncertain hopes. Ah, well, I know as little, maybe even less."

"Do you really mean what you say?" asked the journalist. "Please forgive me, I do not doubt your word. But Victor Dreyel's presentiments, which you call vague, turned out to be well founded. He is dead, but the same danger threatens you."

"The danger of being murdered, do you mean? What for?"

"For being the owner of a wooden image of the same mysterious character as the one owned by your cousin."

"Oh, you stick to that?"

"Of course. Perhaps you doubt your cousin's letter?"

Christian Dreyel hesitated for a few minutes, then he took out a bunch of keys and opened an old-fashioned writing-table which stood behind him.

"No, you are right," he said. "Here it is." And he set a dark, brown wooden figure on the table beside the other one. At first sight they seemed as much alike as two tin soldiers, but Wallion detected a difference; the one he had brought with him featured Victor Dreyel, whereas this second one represented a thin, sinewy man, with small, shifty eyes, a broad hook-nose, and a short goatee.

The journalist examined it closely, and on the sole of one foot he found, as he expected the figures

No. 6
29"

Christian Dreyel, who had been watching him, said with a laugh:

"Oh, yes, they are there sure enough, the figures are in their place. I'll save your making inquiries. I got this thing in a parcel by post at the same time my cousin got his. The parcel came from Seattle in the United States.

There was no explanation with it, and I can't make out the meaning of the figure itself or what the numbers refer to. I wrote to Victor about it and we came to the conclusion that the riddle was impossible to solve."

The honest ring of his voice left no room for doubt, and Wallion's hopes dwindled; his journey had been in vain; the key to the problem was certainly not in Christian Dreyel's hands. Greatly disappointed he pushed the dolls away from him and said:

"So you will not even venture a guess that these figures were sent by William Robertson?"

Dreyel shrugged his shoulders.

"What's the use of guessing? ... I can give you one hint though, the expression 'likeness' of the 'dead' which my cousin used, is quite correct. The figure standing there is meant to represent a certain Aaron Payter, the one my cousin had was meant, he affirmed; for one Walter Randolph ... both Payter and Randolph died fifteen years ago ... we had been schoolfellows..."

Wallion put his hands to his head in despair.

"I don't follow you," he said. "You say you don't know anything, and all the time I feel that I am on the verge of being enlightened. All those names: William Robertson, Craig Russel, Sanderson, the black Colonel, Payter, Randolph and Toroni ... the thirteenth. Who are they? You must know if you were at school together."

He went round to the other side of the table and suddenly taking Dreyel by the shoulders, he said in a tone of annoyance:

"One thing, at least, you can tell me, what is the meaning of King Solomon?"

Dreyel gently but firmly shook himself free. "You are very insistent, Mr. Wallion."

"It concerns more people than yourself."

"You want me to rake up the most terrible recollection of my life. That is asking rather a lot."

"But not too much; can't you understand that I want to help you? What was it that happened fifteen years ago?"

Dreyel had withdrawn a little, but Wallion followed him. "Quick, there's no time to lose. What was ..." he broke off, went up to the table and blew out the light. The room was pitch dark, the window only looked like a pale gray square. A slight rustle in the grass outside had made itself heard, and a figure was dimly discernible running across the garden at lightning speed.

"He has come," whispered Wallion. "You were wrong to doubt. Victor Dreyel's murderer is here now to fetch the other doll."

He adjusted his Browning and opened the window, but it was impossible to distinguish anything among the trees. He turned back into the room and asked in a low voice: "Have you any servants here?"

"No."

"Are all the doors and windows shut and fastened?"

"Yes."

They listened for a few minutes. Nothing could be heard but Christian Dreyel's deep breathing; the tension was beginning to affect Wallion's nerves. He knew that he was not mistaken; the man who had murdered Victor Dreyel, wounded Elaine Robertson, and slipped through the cordon of police in 30, John Street, had come to complete his secret work on the body of the other Dreyel.

The whites of Christian Dreyel's eyes shone in the dark. He had taken a double-barrelled gun from the wall. His powerful frame seemed to grow larger, for the approach of danger seemed to have put new life into him.

"Do you see him?" he whispered.

"No," replied Wallion who, by this time, had jumped out of the window and was standing in the high grass waiting. "You stay there, I'll go after him."

The mysterious shadow had gone past the window from left to right and Wallion carefully took the same direction. Having gone about a dozen steps he stopped to listen; the grass under his feet rustled like silk and he thought he heard a similar rustle a little way off, near the maple trees which sheltered the house on the north. He strained his eyes, but could distinguish nothing, and all was quiet again. Then he suddenly saw before him footprints in the still wet grass ... He started ... The shape of these footprints reminded him of the one he had seen on the chair in Dreyel's studio. That the "Invisible One" had gone this way there was no longer any doubt. The wild beast was near, prowling after his prey, and following him up unalarmed by the hunter. Maurice Wallion crept close to the wall where the path was clear and sprang noiselessly to the corner, half expecting a collision, but a cold shiver ran down his back as he looked ahead; for on the north side of the house there was a door evidently leading to the kitchen, and that door stood wide open ... the ruffian had forced his way into the house. For a moment Wallion was seized with desperate anger. Perhaps the door had not been properly locked. What a mistake, what an unpardonable blunder! He had a vision of Christian Dreyel alone in the room in the dark with the two wooden figures waiting ... for what...?

Wallion uttered a shrill cry of warning and rushed through the open door like a whirlwind. "Look out!" he screamed, "the assassin has got in!"

He ran along a short passage, opened a door and found himself in the front hall. On the right he noticed the door by which Christian Dreyel had let him in. He burst it open and rushed in with his Browning cocked. The window was still open and the curtains waved gently in the breeze, but Christian Dreyel had disappeared!

"Where are you?" he cried. There was no answer; but he thought he heard a faint sound under the window; in three bounds he was there, and stumbling over something soft he fell forward against the window frame.

A stooping, thin, nimble figure was running from tree to tree in the garden and, without more ado, Wallion pulled the trigger and fired. The apparition vanished. He lighted a match and looked down on the ground. He half expected what he saw, but could not repress an exclamation of horror and pity at what the burning match revealed. The object over which he had stumbled proved to be Christian Dreyel's right arm, the man lay motionless on his back under the window, his double-barrelled gun a short distance away. When Wallion raised him up he saw a stream of blood dyeing his shirt red on the left side and found a freely bleeding wound immediately under the collar bone. Dreyel opened his eyes and looked vacantly round.

"The wooden doll," he whispered, "the shadow came up to the table, I saw him ... he stabbed me..."

He pulled himself up into a sitting posture and laid his hands on his breast; it was wet with blood.

"Who fired?" he asked quite confused.

"I did, but the fellow got away. Be careful now, I will put on a bandage and fetch the doctor."

"No, don't ... look after the wooden doll first." The wounded man repeated the words over and over again: "The wooden doll ... the wooden doll..."

Wallion took a cushion from the sofa and put it under Dreyel's head; then he closed the window, drew the curtains and casting one more searching look out into the darkness, went back. To pursue the murderer without help would be worse than useless; he was probably already a long way off.

It had all happened with lightning speed and as he relit the lamp Wallion's hands still trembled from the shock. The chimney was still warm.

He looked at the table where lately two wooden figures had stood. There was now only one—the doll belonging to Christian Dreyel was gone. Wallion took up the one he had brought with him and examined it. Victor Dreyel's image was uninjured; the criminal had passed it over as worthless ... but why ... why...?

"The wooden doll," stammered the wounded man who had fallen back again on the cushion. "It is gone ... he has taken it...."

"Yes," answered Wallion with a great effort at restraint, "once more he has had good luck; but try to be calm, the police will soon get hold of him; you must think of yourself now and only rest."

He bent over the huge form and undid its garments; the blood streamed from the gaping wound, and the laboured breathing showed that the lungs had been touched. Wallion stopped the bleeding with a towel dipped in water, and put on a temporary bandage.

"Send for Doctor Moving," said Dreyel, groaning and twisting under Wallion's touch. "It does burn so ... The devil ... but it must be true he knew that ... King Solomon's secret..."

"I will fetch the doctor myself, lie still," said Wallion in a tone of command. He hurried out into the road on his way to the station, but a few yards from the gate he met a barefooted boy of about ten, coming along with a fishing-rod and a few fish. Wallion took out a florin and put it into the boy's hand.

"Run along to Doctor Moving's and ask him to come here, Captain Street, at once," he said. "At once, do you understand? Mr. Dreyel is ill."

The boy nodded his tousled head, looked at the coin and was off like a shot. Wallion went back to the house. He was pale with excitement; his nostrils quivered and his eyes burned. He was fuming over with what he called his "clumsiness" but a hasty examination of the back door reassured him in some degree, for two or three scratches round the lock showed that it had been forced open by the intruder... So it had been locked, and so far there had been no negligence. He lighted a cigar to soothe his nerves, the tension of which had prevented his being able to think clearly. Through loss of blood the wounded man was sinking into a kind of stupor, but when Wallion gave him a few drops of water he opened his eyes and muttered:

"Now I understand everything ... I see clearly ... Robertson and Toroni have been here... King Solomon... Oh, my God, and that after fifteen years!" He beat the air with his hands and cried with a deep, choking voice: "I saw him as he lifted the knife... I saw him... I saw..."

"All right, but you must be quiet now."

"No, I will speak out. He was greatly changed but I knew him again. It was Toroni."

"What? You yourself told me he was dead."

"No, Toroni ... No, thirteen Toroni ... what a long way off you are ... you don't hear me."

It was tragic and pitiful to see the big, strong man exert the last of his remaining strength in the effort to tell everything, for though the delirium of fever gripped him inch by inch, his lips continued to move and Wallion bent over him to catch his words, low as the beating of his pulse.

"The numbers ... the numbers ... it is from Robertson ... you must help ... many will be grateful to you ... if you can find King Solomon, the numbers ... take care ... I am falling ... take care, Toroni."

He stopped, but his eyes sought the other's with an expression so appealing, so helplessly pitiful that Wallion, deeply touched, pressed his hand.

"I promise to do my best," he said. "Don't distress yourself any more, everything will be all right."

Christian Dreyel smiled like a child and lay still. He closed his eyes, his muscles relaxed and he lost consciousness.

Out in the road the sound of cycle wheels became audible and some one came in through the gate. It was Doctor Moving, and Wallion met him half-way. The doctor was stout of build, getting gray, and had a glowing cigar in his mouth. A few words sufficed to acquaint him with the nature of the case. Without speaking he threw off his coat and helped to carry the man into the bedroom. There, with deft and practised hands the doctor quickly got to work. Fifteen minutes later, he removed the cigar from his mouth and said:

"The fellow has an iron constitution, he has lost a lot of blood, but the wound is not very serious and he will live. The top of one lung is pierced, but it might have been worse. Have you a match?"

"How long will it take him to recover?" said Wallion.

"Well, well, you seem in a hurry," growled the doctor, relighting his cigar. "For the next few weeks he must neither move nor talk, then we shall see. A stab with a knife dealt by such a fiendish expert does not heal at once; but leave him to me, I'll take him under my charge ... You look after the man who dealt the blow."

Wallion shook hands with the doctor, gave one more look at Christian Dreyel's white face and then went away; but he did not forget to put the wooden doll into his pocket. Twenty minutes later, he despatched the following telegram to the Chief Detective in Stockholm:

"This evening Victor Dreyel's murderer attacked Christian Dreyel. Badly wounded. Similar wooden figure stolen. Local police informed. Police dogs needed.—Wallion."

For many years Maurice Wallion had been in possession of a police pass, which was of immense use to him now. Within an hour a thorough, systematic search of the environs had been organized, telephones were working with feverish haste, and the train service at Borne and the surrounding stations put under the strictest surveillance. The following answer from Stockholm reached Wallion at 10:30 A.M.:

"Police dog last train from Gävle. Sustain search thoroughly. Aspeland arriving tomorrow."

* * * *

At midnight a detective from Gävle arrived with a police dog which was led to the marks of the footsteps under the window in Captain Street, and after a short delay took up the scent through the garden. Wallion, the sergeant and detective followed, greatly excited. The dog led them straight through the wood for two miles or more to a high road where he stopped abruptly. He had lost the scent and nothing would induce him to go on. Not far off was a farm and the inmates were called up, but none of them could remember having seen a stranger on the road, although various farm-hands had driven past at quite a late hour. This information inspired the three men with serious misgivings ... The murderer had probably continued his flight concealed in one of those waggons and was, most likely, miles away by this time. The detective from Gävle looked at Wallion and remarked: "I wonder whether an accurate description would not be of rather more use than the dog under present circumstances. Shadow, last seen in a garden, etc., is, anyway, a somewhat dubious clue!"

CHAPTER 7

DOCTOR AUGUSTUS N CORMAN
INTRODUCES HIMSELF

On the morning of the third of August, Aspeland, imbued with more than his usual amount of energy, came rushing into Tom Murner's apartments.

"Have you heard what has happened to Maurice Wallion?" he cried, whilst still on the threshold. "My goodness, he does manage to be on the spot when wanted." Aspeland then related what had taken place in Captain Street on the previous evening, adding "The man is an out and out scoundrel, bold and determined, it remains for us to see that he does not escape our net this time." Breathing hard the superintendent twirled his mustache.

"The wretch may be back in Stockholm by now."

"No, he'll try to get here, no doubt, but today, every train from the north is being watched, and presently I shall be going myself to Gävle. I'm almost sure he has got out of the country; we have no criminal of that type here just now, for he's an expert, he is. Naturally, he would try to get back with his booty on the first available opportunity. Wooden doll, indeed!" The superintendent shook his head. "One man killed and another badly wounded, and all for the sake of getting at a couple of small wooden images. It's more than one can understand."

Aspeland gone, the house once more became as silent as the grave.

Tom Murner, thus doomed to solitude and idleness, was unable either to read or work. The strange drama in which he was one of the actors nearly drove him mad. Who was this girl who had claimed his hospitality in such an unaccountable manner? How was the affair going to end?

Early in the afternoon a telegram arrived from Wallion, but it gave him small comfort.

> "Can't return before tomorrow. Make inquiries after a certain person's luggage. If necessary provide other clothes. Prepare for departure.—WALLION."

Tom called Mrs. Toby out of the bedroom and showed her the telegram.

"Yes, surely, that's right enough," Mrs. Toby said in her usual quiet but decisive tone. "She must be got away tomorrow morning at latest, and that can be managed all right. She was awake a little while ago; it seems she left a box of clothes at the Central Station—the receipt was in the pocket of her jacket—and I have sent for it."

Mrs. Toby's presence went a good way towards soothing Tom, she took everything so naturally, with so much practical good sense, it made him laugh. He answered:

"You say that Miss Robertson woke up. Well, what did she say?"

"Nothing. She looked round as if she didn't quite know where she was, and I noticed that she seemed rather frightened at not being able to locate herself. I comforted her, though she was for getting up and going away at once, but she is terribly weak, poor little soul, and now she has fallen asleep again."

"Can't I see her and speak to her?"

Mrs. Toby shook her head, smiled, and returned to her patient.

* * * *

During these days Tom Murner studied the papers with eagerness. Every time he opened one he did so with as much care as one would handle a dead snake. But in 1918 the press concerned itself chiefly with news of the Great War, the latest sanguinary encounter, and it was only in a mid-day edition of August the third that he came upon a short paragraph reporting that the photographer, Victor Dreyel, had been "found dead in his studio on the night of the day before yesterday, under circumstances which pointed to robbery. Examination by the police is proceeding." Maurice Wallion's own paper, the *Daily Courier*, was silent on the subject, and when no further allusion was made to it on the fourth, Tom began to suspect that the "Problem-Solver" had a hand in its suppression. It was a foregone conclusion that the affair would be kept dark for a few days in order that Elaine Robertson's hiding place should not be discovered, which was also the reason why Wallion wished to hasten her departure, for sooner or later, the bomb was bound to explode. It was not that Wallion's conduct perplexed Murner; he knew the journalist would never work in opposition to the police. Had the search for the girl in gray been totally abandoned? Perhaps.

Deep in the morning paper of August the fourth, Tom pored long over the problem without attaining any result. The day had begun fine and sunny and, unconsciously, his optimistic temper was in harmony with the weather. So far all had gone well. If only Wallion would come…. Mrs. Toby looked into the study with a smile and said, "I thought I heard you whistle, sir."

"You did," he replied cheerfully. "And how is our patient today?"

"I'll go and see," she said, as she withdrew with even a broader smile.

After a short interval the door again opened and Tom cried over his shoulder, "Well, how is she?"

"Very well, thank you," replied a soft, melodious voice.

Tom started and turned round; Elaine Robertson stood before him. She was dressed in a simple gown of black silk and her face, framed by her black hair, was white and transparent as after a long illness. She looked at him gravely, in silence, and put out her hand.

"How can I thank you?" she said.

The blood rose to his cheeks, but he took her hand as a matter of course, and said:

"So you made up your mind to come back to life." Then, after a brief silence on both sides he continued. "I hope Mrs. Toby..."

Then a faint color mantled the girl's cheeks also; she sat down on a chair and said:

"Mrs. Toby has told me everything, I myself cannot remember anything. I seem to have awakened from a bad dream." An absent look came into her dark eyes. She sat silent for a while immersed in recollections which made her features appear cold and hard; then she gave a little sigh, raised her eyes and continued: "I can never repay such kindness, I can only express my thanks to all, Mrs. Toby, yourself, and your friend whom I have never seen."

"Maurice Wallion? Oh, he is coming soon, but please don't talk about gratitude."

"Well, well, I don't understand how you could ... why, you don't even know who I am."

"Was that necessary?"

She pointed to her arm, where a lump under the thin silk blouse revealed the bandage. "The man who gave me that wound ... he knew well enough who I was," she said with a sorrowful smile that went to Tom's heart.

"It proves that Victor Dreyel's murderer was no friend of yours," he answered.

"But you ... are you not afraid I might be an adventuress?" she said in a scarcely audible voice.

They looked into each other's eyes, but suddenly she averted her gaze and bent her head.

"No," he answered, "I was never afraid of that."

She rose hurriedly. "If you won't let me express my thanks there is nothing for me but to go," she said.

He wanted to speak, to beg her to tell him everything in strict confidence; to offer her his help; but all he could manage was to say very awkwardly: "Why?"

"I do not wish to add further to my obligation..."

"Why use that word?"

"Because I know so well that for all you have done, it is impossible to..." Here her voice failed her, she could only whisper: "Without your help I should have been lost indeed!"

This time he dared not attempt a reply. The position was embarrassing for both, and both felt that it was too difficult for words. Luckily, Mrs. Toby appeared; she made a wry face when she saw them apparently so quiet and miserable.

"When you've quite done thinking, both of you," she said, "your breakfast is waiting in the smoke-room." Her practical, humorous remark saved the situation. Tom laughed outright and the girl smiled. Mrs. Toby, too at breakfast, over which she presided, pressed them to eat, and led the conversation with so much natural tact and ease as to banish any awkwardness there might have been. When the meal was over and she left them, they continued their discourse, Tom occasionally stealing a furtive glance at the girl. The sun shone on her half-open lips; her complexion was of a pallid, ivory hue, and for the first time he noticed that her clear cut profile had the charm which Botticelli and pre-Raphaelite painters loved to portray. The only ornament she wore was a small, simple gold locket round her neck. "Tell me," said Tom, leaning forward, "how is it that you can speak Swedish and English equally well? At first I took you for an American."

"Why should you take me for an American?"

"Well, haven't you just come from America? And somehow your name sounds rather American."

She gazed at him with wide-open eyes and the characteristic little frown appeared on her brow as if she were puzzled, but at last she said:

"My father is a Swede, my mother had Swedish blood in her, and Swedish was the language I learnt first."

"Is your father still living?"

"Yes."

"And is his name William Robertson?"

Again she hesitated with her answer, but nodded assent. She cast a troubled look round as if she feared further questioning; then she took off her locket, opened it, and passed it across to Tom.

"That is my father," she said shyly.

It was evidently the work of an amateur, and represented the three-quarter face of an elderly, careworn man; two bright, deep-set eyes shone under a lofty forehead; the hair was white and smooth, the lips were firmly set and the expression of the mouth was as kindly as that of the eyes, which spoke plainly of hopes crushed and a life wasted. Tom was greatly moved. In the old man's countenance were depicted physical suffering and mental worry, yet he seemed to detect a certain likeness to it in the girl by his side, the same melancholy touch of resignation and the same spirit. He reverently closed the locket and gave it back to her ... he understood her trust in him.

"How he must have suffered!"

"He is not even fifty," she replied.

Tom made an involuntary gesture of surprise. The portrait represented him as a man of nearly seventy, one who had turned his back upon life.

"Victor Dreyel was much older," he observed thoughtfully, "but he, too, had that same expression of hopeless resignation."

"They were schoolfellows," said Elaine. "My father..." She stopped; it seemed as if every attempt to speak out or to explain entailed an almost superhuman effort, and as her mute appealing look was more than he could bear, Tom sat down by her side and took her white, trembling hands in his.

"Your father sent you here, did he not?" he said with emotion. "We know that your errand had some connection with those wooden dolls. Victor Dreyel is no more and, I daresay, Mrs. Toby has told you that his cousin has been badly wounded."

Elaine gave a melancholy little nod.

"Both dolls have been stolen. You must see that your errand is too hard for you to accomplish singlehanded; won't you trust yourself to us?"

As she made no answer he continued with some eagerness: "I am not thinking of myself, but I want you to understand about Maurice Wallion and who he is, the best helper you could have, if only you would confide in him...."

"Mrs. Toby has told me about him," replied the girl in a low voice; "Oh, yes, I owe a full explanation to you both ... I can't do anything more by myself." She rose, and withdrawing her hands from his, she cried:

"If only your friend will help me." The cry came from the depth of a burdened heart.

Neither of them had heard the bell or the opening of the door, but at that moment Mrs. Toby appeared and called Tom out.

Maurice Wallion, in traveling get-up, came forward smiling. They shook hands, and Tom's eyes looked searchingly for news.

"I have come direct from Gävle," said Wallion. "Aspeland also returned by the same train. We have had monstrous bad luck; the search has been carried on day and night ... without result."

"Has he escaped again, then?" asked Tom.

"Yes, he wiggled out of the net like an eel, and you may believe me this time we used tempting bait to catch our fish. Did you get my wire?" His angular features simply beamed with pent up energy, and he was evidently much excited as he spoke.

Tom vouchsafing no answer, he resumed:

"Is our client ready to give information? She must get away from here but if she can't give a clear account of herself, the situation is, of course, untenable. One of the boys belonging to the evening paper hangs on to Ferlin like his shadow. Hallo!" he said, turning and bowing to the girl. "I am delighted to see you have returned from the land of feverish dreams."

He took a chair and continued, "You know who I am, don't you? Well, then you will understand that I have something to tell you, so don't be alarmed, and forgive me if I plunge into the thick of it at once ... even the minutes are precious. You cannot remain here, and before we decide upon the next move you must tell us everything."

The girl sat stiff and pale.

"Everything?" she said, solemnly looking up at him. Curiously enough Wallion's quick, energetic manner upset her much less than Tom's more gentle questioning. In a steady voice she at once added:

"And if I refused to say anything?"

"About whom?" asked Wallion kindly.... "Are you referring to your father? In that case he ought to have come himself instead of exposing you to such a dangerous adventure."

Elaine's hand went up to the locket as if it needed protection.

"You don't understand," she said. "I simply had to go ... my father is ill."

"Ill?"

"Yes, he is staying with a friend of ours, Doctor Corman."

"Where?"

"At his private Home, just outside Seattle."

Wallion started visibly and exchanged a quick glance with Tom.

"In a Home, you say. Tell us more about it."

Elaine handed him the locket. He looked closely at the photograph, and she said in a broken voice:

"There you see my father, but you must not think ... you must not think that his mind is affected ... he has broken down with grief and sorrow, no one has gone through so much adversity, but he is not out of his mind."

Wallion returned the locket but said nothing. She pressed it to her bosom and repeated: "He has broken down, but he is not mad, he has been injured by wicked people ... if I had not looked after him he would have died ... Oh, it is only justice he wants and a clear explanation, an explanation of the great, big secret."

She rose and walked to the window, and they saw her furtively drying her eyes.... After a pause she said in a firmer tone:

"I am given to understand you did not hand me over to the police because you wanted to give me an opportunity to explain first. What I tell you now I could not have said before those officials. I came here with the object of getting back from Victor and Christian Dreyel the two wooden dolls given them by my father."

"My dear young lady," replied Wallion, surprised, "we have been aware of that all along, and why wouldn't you give this simple explanation before the officials?"

"Because I am so afraid of those dolls."

"Afraid?"

"Yes, because I can't make out what they are intended for," she said almost inaudibly.

Maurice Wallion leapt from his chair. "You don't know? You? You don't know the secret of those wooden figures for which men have risked their lives and which have apparently vanished into space…. You don't know what the numbers mean, nor what 'King Solomon' is supposed to stand for?"

"No," she replied, and when Wallion, leaning over the table, looked inquiringly into her eyes, she gently added: "I swear that I know nothing."

Wallion stood motionless as if he had received a blow; he fumbled about in his pockets for a cigar and growled: "Nobody seems to know anything—it is inconceivable—neither Dreyel nor you ... and yet that dread of the wooden dolls ... that unreasonable terror." He took sundry whiffs and then in an off hand manner he asked: "And who is Toroni?"

Elaine did not seem to have heard his question; she was leaning out of the window, gazing down the street with wide open eyes. Presently a look of doubt and confusion cast a shadow over her face. She drew back hastily and walked into the room with uncertain steps, gave a shy glance round and said in a totally altered tone: "Don't ask me any more questions, it is no use."

Wallion went to the window and saw an empty motor drawn up at the door; he frowned savagely.

"What did you see?" he asked.

She replied in the same peculiar voice: "I must be going." She spoke as if she were dreaming and her gestures were those of a somnambulist.

"He has come to fetch me."

"He ... who?"

There was a ring at the door and the girl sank trembling into a chair. Mrs. Toby came in with a visiting card in her hand which she gave to Tom. On it he read:

Augustus N. Corman, M.D.
Seattle, U.S.A.

"Doctor Corman requests an interview with you, sir," she said. "He is in the study." She cast a look he knew of old at Wallion and when he was quite close to her, she said in a low voice which he alone could hear: "I have seen him before, he went past the house both last night and this morning and looked up at the window. He speaks English with an American accent."

Wallion nodded and laid a finger on his lips as Tom was about to speak. They both looked at the girl, who sat with her face buried in her hands; she seemed more ashamed than alarmed at having been caught ... a child's mortification. Wallion smiled grimly.

"Come along," he said, going into the study with Tom.

A well-dressed man of middle stature, perfectly self-possessed and at his ease, stood near the table, hat in hand. He was apparently about forty years of age, with a broad forehead and dark brown, wavy hair and mustache, but the eyes behind the gold rimmed pince-nez were clear and blue like billows of the sea, steadfast and piercing; he bowed slightly, saying:

"Good morning, Mr. Murner," in a strong, full voice, as, ignoring Wallion, he looked straight into Tom's face. The latter returned the greeting with a stiff inclination of the head.

"Good morning, Doctor Corman," he said in English ... "This is my friend and adviser, Mr. Wallion."

The Doctor bowed again with perceptibly heightened interest.

"To what do we owe the honor of a visit from you?" Tom said with an effort.

The Doctor's mustache concealed a faint smile of amusement.

"I have come to relieve you from a situation which is certainly as embarrassing as it was unexpected, Mr. Murner."

His sonorous voice was calculated to break down any kind of opposition and to negative any doubts, as a physician's is wont to do in a sick room. Tom felt that the doctor knew all.

"I don't quite understand," he said haltingly.

Doctor Corman waved his hat towards the smoking-room and said: "I have come to take the little lady back to her father. She has had adventures enough. The thing is settled."

"Speak a little more explicitly," he said.

The doctor removed his pince-nez and looked at him with his eyes half-closed, as is the way of people afflicted with short sight.

"Any further explanation between us would be superfluous. I have ascertained that Elaine Robertson is here. I am her guardian, appointed as such by reason of her father's dementia. As such I tender you my thanks for the shelter you have given her and I intend to take her away immediately; my motor is waiting."

Wallion reflected for a while. He gave Tom a meaning look, for here undoubtedly was a step towards the solution of the problem. In any case the girl must go, for this aggressive and amazing doctor was certainly in the right.

"So you affirm that her father is out of his mind?" he asked; "will you not give us a little more information?"

"Do you know what 'Phantom-Mania' is?" answered the doctor. "Delusions about mysteries which are non-existent ... a fear of pursuers who are not there ... a love for sending messages and gifts which mean nothing. Only the overwrought brain of a neurotic girl can give credence to these. The actions of a weak-minded man or the whims and fancies of a nervous young woman ... both have a fictitious value."

"The death of Victor Dreyel, the stab in the girl's arm, the attack in Captain Street and the theft of the wooden dolls were not delusions."

"I am not concerned with what has occurred here. Elaine accidentally crossed the path of an unknown robber ... it is always the unexpected which happens and such contingencies are from the devil."

"Is that all you have to say about it?"

"Yes, I know what I am talking about, Mr. Wallion, and I don't allow myself to be caught unawares. I am here in the capacity of William Robertson's medical adviser and Elaine's guardian, and I desire to see her at once." His tone had a touch of increased sharpness in it.

"One moment," said Wallion, "how did you get here?"

"That is very simple, as soon as Elaine started from Seattle on her imaginary quest, her father grew anxious and in a lucid moment confessed to me that he had acted on a delusion. I set off immediately to prevent the girl from doing anything foolish. My sister, Madame Nina Lorraine, is with me to look after things. The whole affair is a farce, but likely to end in a tragedy."

Wallion laughed and looked straight at the doctor.

"Do you know," he said, "why Miss Elaine is in hiding here? Are you aware that the police are looking for her?"

The doctor gave no answer. The door of the smoking-room slowly opened and Elaine stood on the threshold, pale and silent.

"What are you talking about?" she said in a monotonous tone. "I am here, take me home to father, Doctor Corman, I am so tired."

Corman took her hand with an air of triumph and speaking over her bowed head he said: "There, you see, Mr. Wallion. What are you going to do?"

Wallion replied: "I presume you and your sister are staying in some hotel?"

"Yes, at the Grand Hotel."

"Miss Robertson is quite at liberty to go with you. For the present any further discussion is unnecessary, but what I said just now was meant as a caution to you, doctor, and you shall hear from me before you leave."

"All right," said the doctor frigidly.

Five minutes later, Elaine Robertson had left No. 30 John Street, in Doctor Corman's company.

CHAPTER 8

ONWARD TO THE UNKNOWN

Tom was raving. Everything had been done in such haste that his brain was in a whirl when he tried to look back upon recent events. Elaine's cold and hurried "Good-by" stung him like a thousand pin-pricks, and the doctor's voice echoed fiendishly shrill in his ears. Why had Wallion given in so quickly?

The journalist did not stop to listen to Tom's excited inquiries. He made some hurried notes in his pocket-book and departed. It seemed as if he were pursuing some new train of thought. Had he got weary of the Elaine Robertson mystery after the unforeseen intermezzo? Half-an-hour later, he sent the following telephone message: "Expect me at five o'clock. Tell Mrs. Toby to have dinner ready and inquire whether any one saw the girl leave the house. Further details later on." Then he rang off.

* * * *

Shortly before five o'clock that same afternoon Wallion came to see Tom, who was sitting in his room, lost in melancholy reflections.

"We have hurled the bomb," he said, throwing a bundle of newspapers on the table, "but it has not exploded yet."

He proceeded to unfold the evening paper and pointed to a column therein, headed:

ASSASSINATION OF DREYEL. AN ACT OF REVENGE.

Christian Dreyel also attacked and robbed.
Two Works of Art stolen. Was it the act
of a madman?

"Now listen," said Wallion, laughing. "My colleague of the evening paper has been very energetic, the last paragraph is of most interest to us," and he began to read:

"The unknown young lady who left Victor Dreyel's studio at the time of the murder has not made herself known; she is now said not to have been implicated. She may have been a casual customer come to fetch her photographs, or an acquaintance of the murdered man's, and on the presumption that she found him lying dead it was only natural that she should have declined to come forward as a witness, and her depositions would not, anyhow, have been more reliable than those of the porter's wife. It has been ascertained that the perpetrator was a man who set about his dastardly work with unusual—one may say, incredible—brutality, and the fact that his sole aim both in John Street and in Captain Street was to get at a certain statuette, a bit of carved wood of little value, proves that the scoundrel must have been a maniac, perhaps actuated by a feeling of revenge towards the Dreyels, who during their long residence abroad, etc., etc...."

"Well made up," said Wallion, stopping abruptly. "A wonderful mixture of truth and falsehood. Special stress must be laid on the fact that the girl in grey is done with, that she no longer counts. The *Daily Universal* actually doubts the porter's wife being in her right senses; whereas the *Evening News* exhorts the unknown lady in any case to come forward and to affirm that she was out of it all! The chief point at present, however, is that, now the papers have taken it up, the girl in grey has vanished like smoke. I have just been to the Police Court and seen Ferlin, who was as subdued and crestfallen as a whipped hound, for he has been wild to catch her all the time. What would he have said if he had been here and seen the doctor drive away with her in his car? By-the-bye..." he looked inquiringly at Tom, who replied:

"No, no one noticed Miss Robertson going away. She was dressed in black, and even the porter's wife had not curiosity enough to come up."

"Good," said Wallion, rather relieved. He looked scrutinizingly at Tom Murner's downcast face and intuitively guessed what he was thinking of.

"Don't look so glum," he said. "I don't deny that Doctor Corman cropped up rather inopportunely, but I should never have dreamt of preventing him. All he said was perfectly clear and explanatory..."

"Explanatory?" said Tom, scornfully; "when he refused to give any information, pooh-poohing everything as if it were a fable?"

"Just so, Doctor Corman is an interesting personality, perhaps more interesting than you think. I have heard sundry details, so listen to what I am going to tell you. Corman and his sister arrived late on the evening of the first of August and went to the Grand. Therefore he came at the same time as Miss Elaine, whom he wanted to 'overtake'; they travelled in the same train from Gothenburg and in all probability on the same steamer from America. Do you understand that? During the entire journey, therefore, he must have been more or less near her, but he did not reveal his identity until today; and— what is even more remarkable—he had not only bespoken rooms for himself and Madame Lorraine, but for Miss Elaine Robertson as well."

"What is that you say?" interrupted Tom, half dazed; "I don't take it in. Do you mean to imply that the doctor and the girl acted in collusion?"

"Not at all. At first I thought so, but that is very unlikely. No, the doctor kept at a distance to see what she was up to. Wait a minute, I can see what you are thinking about; no, old man, the doctor is not identical with Victor Dreyel's murderer or the marauder of Captain Street. The latter I saw with my own eyes and his build was quite different; he was much shorter and thinner. Besides, the doctor only left the hotel for a few hours and could not possibly have been anywhere north of Gävle, but he has very frequently been out here. We must take care not to confound him with the miscreant unless we have incontestable proofs. So far he is immune. Note that the girl seemed to trust him, and was quite ready to go with him."

At this juncture Tom again burst out into vituperation.

Wallion listened unperturbed, but at last he spoke:

"Why did I let her go? Because just when Corman turned up I recognized the difficulty of our position; we were not justified in keeping her here. When the girl showed herself willing to go with him, the affair was 'settled,' as the doctor expressed it. But it is not at an end yet."

He sat down and seemed to be ruminating. After a while Tom heard him mutter to himself: "Anyhow, he is most interesting as a representative of a certain type."

"Who? Doctor Corman?" interrogated Tom.

Wallion vouchsafed no reply; he had suddenly grown taciturn, sullen, almost irritable, and soon after dinner he went out, taking Mrs. Toby back with him as her services were no longer required at No. 30, John Street. Tom remained alone in the little dwelling which now seemed to him gloomy and deserted, not to say haunted.

* * * *

Next day came the long expected summons from the Chief Detective, which he obeyed with considerable misgivings, but the Chief received him very pleasantly, and the cross-examination was reduced to a few questions regarding his connection with Victor Dreyel, though he was asked to furnish a minute description of the famous wooden doll.

"Do you know Mr. Wallion?" the Chief finally inquired with a long, searching look at Tom.

"Yes," the latter replied. "It was through me that he came to take an interest in this business."

"H—m! It's odd that he never published the results in the *Daily Courier*. Do you know whether he intends to continue his investigations?"

"No," answered Tom, not without a touch of annoyance, for it was a question he had been debating with himself all the morning.

"Well," said the Chief in a genial manner, "remember me to Mr. Wallion, and tell him, if he hears news that might lead to important results we shall be happy to coöperate with him."

When Tom reached home he found Wallion sitting in his study, with the wooden doll on the table in front of him, and looking rather disconcerted. As Tom entered he said:

"Look here, we forgot this thing when we gave Miss Elaine back her satchel, and she will know that we searched it."

Tom proposed that it should be sent to the Grand at once.

"It is too late, Doctor Corman and the two ladies have gone to Gothenburg."

"What? Already?"

"Yes, and they have booked their passages on the next boat to America ... it leaves on Thursday next week."

Tom could see that Wallion had something up his sleeve by the dry way in which he spoke, and the suspicion caused him to look fixedly at his friend.

Maurice Wallion sat still with his eyes half-closed, his hands in his pockets.

"Maurice," asked Tom impatiently. "What are you thinking about?"

"What did the Chief say?" was Walloon's retort.

Tom repeated the conversation and gave his message.

Wallion laughed. "Results?" he said. "There is only one way to get any 'results' in this affair."

"What might that be?" queried Tom.

Wallion opened his eyes very wide and said:

"It is to allow Elaine Robertson and Doctor Corman to continue their journey unmolested."

"Back to Seattle?"

"Yes, and to follow in their track to the same place."

Tom clung to the arm of his chair for support; they looked at each other in silence for some minutes.

"Since Doctor Corman took Elaine under the shelter of his wing, there is only one place where this conundrum can be solved, and that place is a certain private 'Home' or asylum on the outskirts of Seattle."

"But what about the other ... the murderer?"

"Something tells me that the police will never capture him here, but that he himself and the two dolls will be found at the journey's end."

Wallion spoke with a sort of wistful longing. Tom could not refrain from looking at him earnestly; he began to think he had but half-known his friend so far. A craving for action took possession of him also; and when at last he grasped the portent of Wallion's look the "Problem-Solver" had come to a decision.

"At the end of the journey?" repeated Tom, in a voice which shook with excitement ... "Are you going?"

"I promised Christian Dreyel I would do my best," replied Wallion.

The two men exchanged glances which furnished a sufficient answer to the perplexed thoughts of many clays. Great resolutions are not necessarily preceded by much talking.

"I shall go with you," said Tom.

"I knew you would," was Wallion's laconic reply.

* * * *

The newspapers had not succeeded in stirring up any great interest in the Dreyel case, and when the novelty had worn off, they said no more about it. After Victor Dreyel's funeral, which took place on the Monday following, Wallion had a short conversation with Aspeland in the deserted studio. The Superintendent was reluctantly giving up his hopeless task and said somewhat bitterly:

"Toroni is merely a name. We have done our utmost, but we can't put the bracelets on a shadow, and the search is at an end unless something new turns up."

Wallion and Aspeland left the studio together, and the latter having locked up and given the keys to the porter, wended his way home.

"A symbolical proceeding," remarked Wallion to Tom a little later.

"Victor Dreyel has solved the great riddle and has gone 'home'; Aspeland found no clue, and he has gone 'home' ... it is our turn now, No. 13 Toroni."

Wallion and Tom started for Gothenburg on the following Tuesday. Tom wished to defray the traveling expenses, but Wallion, after his work in England, was financially independent, and settled matters with these words:

"War expenses have to be shared equally ... Danger and success likewise ... Is that clear to you now? Well then, off and away to the great unknown."

PART II

"THE WOODEN DOLLS"

CHAPTER 9

ELAINE ROBERTSON'S STORY

"Our second day on board and not a glimpse of either her or the doctor," said Tom, gloomily. "I begin to doubt their being on board at all."

He and Wallion were standing on the promenade deck, leaning over the rails, and by chance no one else was there. For two days the gigantic propeller had been plowing its way through the surf. A fresh breeze was blowing and the sky stretched like a blue canopy from horizon to horizon across the ever rising and falling waves. The rhythmical thud of the machinery within the capacious interior of the boat reached them where they stood.

Tom gazed at the endless amplitude of the ocean, and, obsessed by doubts when Wallion did not reply, at once continued. "After all what are we really here for? Who knows whether the solving of the mystery connected with those wooden dolls does, indeed, await us? We may have left it behind, and Elaine may have disappeared for ever."

Wallion made a gesture as if lie had just awakened from sleep, and looked at his friend.

"Compose yourself," he said. "You don't suppose I should leave anything to chance? Certainly we did not see them come on board, but they are here. I have seen the list of passengers, and have had a chat with the purser; they have engaged two of the best upper deck cabins. Madame Lorraine and the girl are in number five and the doctor in number seven. As they keep so much to themselves, and even have their meals in the cabin, I fancy they are aware of our presence. I daresay they wonder—perhaps, not without reason, what our intentions are."

"Yes, what must she think?" said Tom gravely. "What shall I say to her?"

"Say to her? Why tell her the truth, that I am going to Seattle on business for Christian Dreyel, and that you have come to keep me company. The promenade deck is free to all, and before this adventure has come to an end I shall have to thank my stars and yours that we were on the spot," said Wallion with much energy.

He threw away his cigar and looked at his watch.

"It is time to dress for dinner; we may meet our interesting traveling companions in the dining-saloon."

"Do you think so?"

"Yes, they will have to get the better of their ... shyness, shall I say? Otherwise one might think they were suffering from a guilty conscience."

When they entered the luxurious, brilliantly-lighted saloon, the two men found themselves among the late comers. Tom took his seat with burning cheeks ... He had seen her again!

Elaine Robertson sat at one of the tables at the farther end. She wore a simple but costly black evening dress, her head was bent but he thought that a slight blush mantled her cheeks also. Had she seen him? Doctor Corman, whose dark, Mephistophelian face expressed nothing in particular, sat on her left. On her right Tom noticed a bright, good-looking woman with thick, burnished golden hair, who at that moment, appeared to be putting a serious question to the Doctor.

"Madame Lorraine," remarked Wallion. "I wonder if she was making any inquiries about us?"

The doctor's face turned in their direction, and he gave his interlocutor a curt answer; for, if he had noticed their presence he certainly did not show it. Tom fidgetted with impatience.

"Don't worry," said Wallion, "we shall naturally get into conversation with them, and don't keep staring their way; there are plenty of other people to look at."

Tom hardly heard him. Wallion continued talking and presently Tom became interested.

"Look at that little man at the small table, on the left there in the corner—the one that looks like an Assyrian,—how does he strike you?"

Tom followed the direction indicated by Wallion and quickly discovered the individual mentioned.

He was a man with narrow shoulders who ate and drank with philosophical complacency, and without speaking to any one. His appearance was calculated to attract attention, his raven black, wavy beard was parted down the middle and formed a sort of shiny chest-protector under the sickly, thin-lipped mouth, above which was a long, straight nose, starting from an abnormally high, arched forehead of triangular shape, fringed by untidy, unkempt black locks, while his eyebrows resembled streaks of soot.

"Who is he?" asked Tom, "a Persian philosopher?"

"No, in the list of passengers he figures as a Greek antiquary; his name is Ricardo Ferail, which does not in the least sound like Greek."

"He seems to interest you?"

"He does, I should rather like to see him run," replied Wallion absently; "but do look at Madame, I believe she is scolding."

Madame Lorraine had moved closer to Doctor Corman, and was talking earnestly to the Doctor who several times shook his head.

Some of those sitting near began to notice them, and Madame stopped talking with an angry shrug of her ample white shoulders.

At that moment something very strange occurred. The Greek antiquary, whose heavy eyelids had until now been cast down on his plate, suddenly raised his dark, velvety orbs and turned them towards Elaine with a sinister, dreamy look. Elaine started visibly as if she had come into contact with some loathsome object, and presently she got up hurriedly, said something to the Doctor and left the saloon.

Corman and his sister exchanged glances and followed her; all three disappeared, but the Greek continued his meal with the same indolent serenity. As Tom was also about to get up, Wallion said: "Sit still, there's no hurry."

"But I want to speak to her," replied Tom, "I don't understand what is going on here, but she looks sad and depressed, and once for all I must speak to her."

"All right," retorted Wallion, "but couldn't you wait a few minutes?"

"And suppose they should retire to their cabins again?" said Tom vexed.

"They won't this time," said Wallion, "that would be a very bad policy, and the Doctor is a thorough diplomat ..."

A quarter of an hour later, Tom and Wallion again came up on deck with fairly buoyant expectations. They had not long to wait for their mysterious fellow-passengers. Doctor Corman came out of the saloon with hands outstretched as if he had only just recognized them.

"What a surprise!" he cried, "the world is very small; so there was some truth in what my sister heard: that the famous Maurice Wallion was on board. We should have met before if the two ladies had not been so sick." He shook them warmly by the hand and talked incessantly as if to make up for the cool and over-hasty leave-taking in John Street.

"So delightful, gentlemen, such a charming surprise ... we can travel in company."

"Yes," said Wallion, "as far as Seattle let us hope."

The doctor's expression of polite surprise, which was undeniably only a mask, became more marked.

"As far as Seattle?" he repeated in an entirely indifferent tone.

"Yes," replied Wallion smiling, "the last time we met I promised that you should hear from me before you left Sweden. We called once or twice at your hotel at Gothenburg, but never had the luck to find you in, so we were obliged to put off asking for the little elucidation we require, until now."

The doctor's eyes became sharper behind his pince-nez.

"Your journey to Seattle seems to have been quite a sudden plan?"

"As sudden as Dreyel's death, Doctor Corman, which makes an explanation all the more needful."

The doctor gave a mocking smile, and said, "Well, my curiosity is beginning to be aroused; let us go into the saloon." He led the way, and before he realized where he was, Tom found himself bowing before Elaine Robertson, whose fearless, serious eyes looked into his. She was sitting beside Madame Lorraine on a sofa in the corner. Tom had an uncomfortable suspicion that this meeting had been pre-arranged.

The doctor introduced his sister, and the usual civilities were exchanged. Madame was stout, unusually fair and good-looking, a little over thirty, with sea-green, sleepy eyes and carmine lips; she looked at the two men with the bold curiosity of a woman of the world but said nothing. Tom took a seat by Elaine and asked:

"Are you not surprised to see us here?"

"No," she said. "I knew you were on board."

"Don't you wonder what brought us here?"

"Well, perhaps ... why should I, though?" she broke off with a smile. "We were bound to meet on the way, were we not?"

"Of course, if one's destination happened to be the same," he replied.

Just then Doctor Corman's voice was heard from above their heads: "And only think, Elaine, what a surprise, these gentlemen are going to keep us company as far as Seattle."

She breathed hard, her dark eyes gazing into the far distance. Turning to Tom, she asked eagerly: "Is that so?"

He nodded assent and turned for confirmation to Wallion, who drew up a chair and joined them. The Doctor sat down by his sister, folded his arms with an air of interested expectation and said pleasantly: "Well, now let us have the little explanation you seem to think so necessary, Mr. Wallion."

"After what occurred in Stockholm the necessity should be patent," replied Wallion. "I consider it my duty to inform you that I am traveling at the request of Christian Dreyel to get a little light upon the mystery of those wooden dolls, and, as we are convinced that it can be obtained only from William Robertson, we desire to see your father in person, Miss Robertson, and rely upon Doctor Corman's assistance."

Elaine never moved but listened with strained attention. The Doctor was going to speak, but Wallion continued:

"Yes, the information you gave us at our former meeting was most valuable, but even for 'Phantom-Mania' there must be some tangible reason, and it is this reason or cause we wish to discover. Is there anything in William Robertson's life to account for the death of Dreyel or the vile attack upon his cousin?"

"You think there is?" said the Doctor very deliberately.

"It is my firm conviction."

In a still more leisurely tone the Doctor said:

"Elaine, would you mind telling these gentlemen how you found your father?"

"No," she answered promptly, with what might have been taken for a sigh of relief. She looked at Wallion and said: "All along I have been anxious to tell you all I knew. There isn't anything I want to keep back ... but a great deal ... oh, such a great deal that I don't understand."

Tom was quite surprised at her evident eagerness, and it had a similar effect upon Wallion. She no longer looked at any one in particular, but was pale and nervous, as if she feared the opportunity might slip away from her, and began her story at once, in a low, subdued voice:

"My father was born in Sweden, for William Robertson is only an alteration of his Swedish name, which he has not used for the last thirty years. The name he bore during his boyhood in Sweden is no longer remembered. The narrow-minded and proud relations who forced him to leave his native land are all gone."

"They forced him?" interposed Wallion.

"Yes," she went on. "Perhaps it is not such an unusual story. His father was a lawyer and wanted his son to become one also. At Upsala he got among the artists, discovered that he had a talent for sculpture, neglected his studies and evil rumors came to the ears of his father. They led to a crisis which ended in his leaving the country precipitately. He has never done wrong to any one, never deceived or slandered others as they have slandered him. He came over to the United States, broken down, without means and, though a well-educated University man, was by turns reporter on a 'gold' paper, barman, steward on a fruit-ship, and lastly a tramp. Then he went out West, and was stableman on a wheat-farm until he became foreman. The owner of the farm, Mr. Bridgeman, took an interest in him, and one day, happening to see a sketch my father had made—a pastoral idyll—sent it to a paper in San Francisco, which accepted it, and, in a few years' time, my father became a popular, well-paid draughtsman. That was his best time. He married Violet Seymour and settled in San Francisco. I was born on January 10, 1898." Here she paused.

The siren over their heads sent a deafening signal out into the night, and was answered by another in the offing. When all was quiet, Elaine again took up the thread of her story:

"On New Year's Day, 1902, my father accidentally came across two Swedes whom he had known from childhood. They were the cousins Dreyel, Victor and Christian, and they told him they were just going to Alaska. At that time Klondyke had not the same old lure, but gold had been discovered in the sand on the shores of the Seward peninsula in 1898, and the two Dreyels met a Scotchman, Sandy MacCormick by name, who professed to know quite a new place for digging the precious metal. When my father heard their glowing promises he, too, was seized with the gold-fever and resolved to join them. He begged my mother to remain in San Francisco, and promised her he would return within a twelvemonth. Then, with the two Dreyels and MacCormick, he set off for Alaska."

"Aha!" ejaculated Wallion, whose eyes were glittering, "you won't object to my jotting down a few notes, will you?"

Almost unconsciously she bent her pretty head in assent and went on:

"That was the last my mother saw of him. In the autumn of the same year terrible news reached us, and though I was only five years old I can remember the beautiful, pale face of my mother on the morning she was found dead in her chair. Something awful must have happened up there in Alaska, but how we got the message or what it was I don't know, only that it was too much for my mother's weak heart. Mr. and Mrs. Bridgeman took me to live with them, and what I have been telling you now was told me by Mr. Bridgeman, but my father's fate was never mentioned. I took it for granted that he was dead. The Bridgemans were kind, superior people; they gave me all they could, and I was devoted to them. But Mrs. Bridgeman—auntie—died when I was sixteen, and Mr. Bridgeman the year following—strange to say of the same complaint—inflammation of the lungs. I succeeded in getting a situation as typist in a business-house in Sacramento."

"Did the Bridgemans leave you anything?" asked Tom.

"No, the farm was entirely in the hands of the railway company, owing to bad harvests for two years in succession. I obtained a better post after a time in an office in Seattle, but did not get on there; one of the directors, Mr. Dixon, who had been advertising for an expert stenographer for his office at Seattle, fortunately chose me, after making the most minute enquiries, from among a hundred applicants, and I have been eighteen months in his employment. Mr. Dixon is one of the leading men of business in Seattle and has, among other things, a wide-spread import connection, while he owns a wharf and several hotels on the coast for summer visitors. He is exacting, but kind and helpful, and he showed great interest in my father's fate. He offered to assist me to send out a search party, but nothing came of it. In November last year..." Elaine leant back on the sofa and closed her eyes, but after a short rest she continued with trembling voice:

"In the beginning of November last year I saw my father again after fifteen years. I found him in a way which you might think beyond belief. One of Mr. Dixon's hotels had been burned down; there were difficulties about the insurance and, as Mr. Dixon was away, it was part of my duty to furnish the reporters with certain details, and that was how my name came to be in all the local papers. A few days later, a white-haired, bent, fever-stricken man walked into the office. He wept for joy, and could hardly articulate my name ... that man..." She looked up, her eyes full of tears ... "that man was my father! He had seen my name in the papers but, scarcely dared believe his eyes, and it was almost ghastly to see his childish delight, for he was completely broken down and was living in the greatest poverty in one of the most squalid quarters in Seattle ... I have shown you his photograph. I had to look after him like a child, and I soon began to notice that he was no longer in full possession of his senses. I could only vaguely surmise that he had returned from Alaska towards the close of the year 1902, ruined and in despair; that when he heard that my mother was dead and I had gone, no one knew where, he was stricken down with a sharp attack of brain fever, and five months later, dismissed from the hospital, a wreck both physical and mental. I dare not even think of the life he must then have led for nearly fifteen years, sunk in melancholy brooding, a lonely wanderer from place to place. I could never prevail upon him to tell me what had happened up there in Alaska, the region of gold and death, which had been the primary cause of his misery and my mother's death; but it must have been something awful, indescribable and terrible, for every question I asked made him shudder, and, at times, when I could see in his eyes that some dread recollection had risen in his mind, he became nearly wild with despair or unreasoning fury, and after such attacks he rarely spoke for days together. More serious symptoms then appeared. He adhered to the idea that spies were on his track; he used to burn paper as a spell, and shut himself up in his room and busy himself with some mysterious work, the nature of which I found out only by slow degrees. He used to carve little wooden figures which he called his dolls, his guardians, and he said:

'Don't you see they watch over certain secrets. They are the dead waiting.'

"His undue excitement made me very anxious, and when Mr. Dixon became aware of that I was obliged to tell him everything. He was greatly touched and made me consult Doctor Corman, who at once pronounced my father to be suffering from 'Phantom-mania.'"

"And that in the worst form," corroborated the Doctor. "I immediately took William Robertson under my own personal observation in my Home, and my diagnosis revealed maniacal tendencies; as frequently happens, he was perfectly sane with regard to the details of every-day life."

A long silence ensued. Then Wallion asked:

"And what is your own impression, Miss Robertson, for you would scarcely undertake a journey from Seattle to Stockholm for the purpose of carrying out a sick man's fancy?"

"I hardly knew what to think," she replied shivering. "A feeling sometimes comes over me that eventually ... that my father..."

"That your father? ... What? ..." queried the doctor.

"I don't rightly know," she stammered. "But if you had seen the look in my father's eyes when he bade me go and bring back the two wooden figures he had secretly sent to the two Dreyel cousins, if you had heard his tearful appeal, you would understand me better. It was one evening early in July that he persuaded me to undertake the journey. 'It is a matter of life or death to your father, Elaine,' he said, 'you must tell them that Toroni has discovered the secret, and you must bring back the wooden dolls, but take good care of them; go alone and speak to no one.' At that moment I thought him not responsible for his words and actions, but I went. I felt that I was fulfilling a duty—abstract, but imperative—I can't express myself more clearly. My father gave me one of the dolls as a sort of pattern."

"And which, I am afraid, we forgot to give you back," said Wallion, laughing.

"I never want to see it again," she answered, with another shiver. "I have told you all I know of the abominable transactions which prevented my getting the dolls, and you know more than I do."

"Only another question or two," said Wallion. "How did your father know the addresses of the two cousins?"

"I believe he was in correspondence with an Information Bureau in Stockholm. Just before being taken to the asylum he indulged in an enormous amount of letter writing to various places."

"Had he told you to send that telegram provisionally to Dreyel from Gothenburg?"

"Yes ... as a warning; he said that every hour might be fatal."

"Extraordinary!" remarked Wallion, looking at Doctor Corman. "Under these circumstances do you really believe the appearance of the assassin to have been accidental?"

The doctor shrugged his shoulders and said nothing.

"Anyhow, you followed the young lady about," said Wallion with some asperity. "You believed there was danger."

"Danger only to this extent, that she had started almost without means, and without protection," retorted the doctor drily. "Forgive me for referring to such a trifling fact, Elaine; your hurried journey was more like an attempt to escape, wasn't it?"

Elaine had risen, she put both hands up to her head and said wearily: "I have a bad headache, and am so tired I think I must go in."

She staggered and leant heavily on Tom's arm. Madame Lorraine rushed to the girl's aid and lovingly took her in her arms.

"My darling," she said fondly, "you have overexerted yourself, and you must go in and rest."

All had risen from their seats. With a wan smile Elaine bade them "Good-night," and obediently went in with Madame Lorraine. When the two ladies had gone there was a gloomy silence for a time, broken at last by Doctor Corman.

"As you see, her nerves are overwrought. I am sorry to have interrupted the interesting recital so abruptly, but, no doubt, you observed that my statement regarding William Robertson's condition was confirmed. Do you still consider your journey to Seattle necessary?"

"A journey begun should never be abandoned," said Wallion sententiously, fixing his eyes upon him.

The doctor threw back his head and laughed, showing his big white teeth. "All right ... I admire your energy, I promise to do what I can to hasten the result ... au revoir!" He bowed and departed.

"Oh, excellent Doctor!" murmured Wallion. "I'll give you an opportunity to keep your promise. Let us go into the smoking-room, Tom."

On the upper deck the Greek antiquary passed close to them and then disappeared like a shadow into the darkness.

CHAPTER 10

RICARDO FERAIL

The next day after dinner Wallion and Tom were quietly sitting in their cabin. The latter in a miserable frame of mind, for Elaine and her people had not appeared at table. He had sent an attendant with his visiting card to inquire after Elaine's health, and was waiting impatiently for an answer. Wallion smoked in silence, casting an occasional glance at his friend.

"Alaska," he suddenly said as though following up a train of thought. "Why shouldn't 'King Solomon' have been the name of a mine?"

"Why not, indeed?" remarked Tom starting up. "But, if so, why did the Dreyels or Robertson not go back there?" he said, hesitatingly. "A mine can't disappear entirely from the face of the earth."

"No, but it can be exhausted, and the booty purloined ... There are all sorts of possibilities in connection with Alaska. I wish we were on land, we might glean some information from the papers of 1902 as to whether there was any catastrophe there at that time, how news of it was conveyed to Mrs. Robertson, what became of Sandy MacCormick, and who Sanderson, and Russel were—to say nothing of the wooden dolls?"

Tom looked uneasily at Wallion, who continued to envelop himself in a cloud of smoke and asked in a low tone:

"What do you think about her story?"

This was the tenth time this question, with sundry variations, had been put to Wallion, but he remained quite unruffled, and answered:

"It is a most extraordinary one ... I have already said I consider it remarkable."

"Just so, but did she tell us the truth? Who on earth is this Doctor Corman, with his sarcastic, satanic countenance?" said Tom. "Maybe he has forced her to ... to..."

"Tell lies? No, her story is incontrovertible, and as far as she knows, perfectly true," said Wallion, leaning forward as he continued:

"But that does not prevent the doctor's demeanor from seeming rather singular. I have just got hold of an interesting tale about their journey from New York to Gothenburg. They traveled on this very boat; Elaine went second class, the Doctor and his sister first class, but did he know then that the fugitive he was pursuing was so near ... or did he not? Again, how could fugitive and pursuer travel in the same train from Gothenburg to Stockholm without noticing one another?"

"Well, that might be possible."

"It might be possible, but it is not likely. People meet so easily on board ship; for instance, I myself am already acquainted with all our fellow passengers, both first and second class, *in every detail*."

Tom burst out laughing.

"And did you find out anything?"

"Yes, I heard who else of those on board her now traveled by this liner on her last voyage to Sweden."

"Well?"

"It seems there is only one other, and his name is Ricardo Ferail."

"The Greek antiquary?"

"Yes."

Tom recalled the look the Greek had given to Elaine in the dining-saloon, and with an uncomfortable kind of foreboding he said:

"Do you know whether they are acquainted with each other?"

"Not openly, at least."

An odd undefined suspicion flitted through Tom's brain. He got up and looked long and fixedly at his friend, but Wallion's features were inscrutable; he was listlessly staring at the ceiling, his hands clasped behind his head. Just then Tom's attention was diverted by a waiter, who handed him a card and disappeared. On the card, and written in a bold round hand, were these words:

"I have ordered our protégée absolute rest for the next few days.
Kindest regards.

"Augustus N. Corman."

"Damn the doctor!" cried Tom. "I don't like his tone. He and Madame Lorraine keep guard over Elaine as if she had committed some crime. Besides who the deuce is this Madame Lorraine?"

"She married a French violin player, Roland Lorraine by name, but they were separated, that's all I know," replied Wallion, getting up from his seat and yawning. "Are you coming in?"

"No," said Tom, throwing himself on the sofa, "as our fellow travelers prefer to remain invisible I can worry here as well as anywhere else."

But when Wallion opened the door to go out, Tom remembered a question he wanted to ask him.

"Why do you wish to see Ferail run, as you said yesterday at dinner?"

Wallion turned back. "Wouldn't it be rather amusing to see an antiquary run?" he answered quite seriously.

Tom winked and threw up his hands. "Get out," he said. "I feel my brain reeling.... God knows what sort of a nightmare I shall have tonight."

The giant liner pursued its appointed way over the ocean; showers of feathery foam played round the bows and all lights were on. From the depths below, between decks, the wind wafted aloft echos of cheerful dance music. A fresh breeze had sprung up and there was no one on deck. Evidently they were enjoying themselves on board.

For the last hour and more, Maurice Wallion had been pacing up and down, his hands thrust deep into his pockets. Now that he was alone his clear cut features looked grave and perplexed; he had been turning the problem over in his mind, and he had just realized that he could acquire full and ir-refutable information on one important detail whenever he felt inclined to do so. He had never found himself in such a peculiar situation; but with a sudden, resolute gesture, he flung the end of his cigar into the water; and as it disappeared in the dark like a shooting star, he muttered to himself: "Yes, I'll do it."

He went down to the promenade deck, and a minute later appeared calm and unperturbed in the smoking-room, which was crowded and blue with smoke. In a corner to the left of the bar, he perceived an Assyrian profile which made him screw up his eyes. It was Ricardo Ferail having a game of poker with three other men. Wallion who, as a rule, recognized every other or every third person he came across in the four quarters of the globe, earnestly scanned Ferail's partners, and found that he knew one of them well. Here was luck. He advanced, and gave the man in question a tap on the shoulder, saying:

"Evening, Mr. Derringer! It's a long time since that night at Johannes-burg."

"So it's you, Mr. Wallion," he answered without a trace of embarrass-ment. Derringer was a thin, bony Englishman with a skin deeply tanned by a tropical sun. "Take a chair and join in our game; we want one more to make up the ideal five."

After a casual, formal introduction to the other players, Wallion sat down. Ferail, who was the dealer, lifted his eyes for a second and gave him a swift look. The play continued for a time without interruption and in silence. Then the Greek ran his fingertips through his frowzy beard, cast down his eyes, and observed:

"Where did you learn to play poker, Mr. Wallion?"

"At an Officers' Mess in India, Mr. Ferail."

"A very fine school, no doubt," said the antiquary. "You are going to beat me."

These were the first words they had exchanged. The game went on. Half-an-hour later, Derringer burst out laughing, and said: "Your luck has turned, eh, Ferail?"

The antiquary had really lost a considerable amount, and his pile of money melted quickly away. Wallion acted on the defensive; he neither won nor lost, but kept his eye on Ferail, who sat sulky and silent, his white face, with the thin, sickly lips, giving not the slightest indication of the workings of his mind. He shuffled the cards and dealt them with a quick and practised hand. He seldom bought more than one or two, and with a kind of dogged obstinacy kept increasing his stakes, but that no longer helped him, for he lost every round. After another ten minutes Derringer rose, and there was no more play.

"It's so deucedly monotonous always to be winning," he said with a yawn. "Let us leave off, I'll give you your revenge tomorrow."

He and his two friends left the saloon, and Wallion and Ferail found themselves alone, sitting opposite one another.

Drops of moisture shone on the Greek's forehead, and he blinked his eyes as, with philosophic composure, he gathered up the cards, but he did not seem conscious that Wallion's sharp eyes were constantly fixed upon him. Presently Wallion leant across the table and said:

"Now to business, please ... No. 13 Toroni."

It seemed ages before Ferail opened his shining black eyes to their full extent and shot an enigmatic glance at Wallion, saying as he did so: "I don't take you."

"Have a little sense, Toroni," said Wallion with an ambiguous smile. "Perhaps you are not used to my ways ... but why should not we two be frank with each other? There are no witnesses!"

"I don't grasp your meaning," repeated Ferail, in the same tone of indifference.

"Well, I'll explain to you. First of all then I'll tell you how I know who you are. My theory is this: In all probability Toroni traveled to Stockholm in the same boat and the same train as Elaine, and both arrived simultaneously at Dreyel's studio; it is equally probable that, having accomplished his object, Toroni immediately returned to America. When one hears that a particular person used the same boat for a voyage there and back, one begins to take an interest in that person, and if he is short, thin and nimble the interest is heightened. *You* are that person, but it has yet to be proved whether you are identical with 'Toroni.' According to Christian Dreyel's account the man I saw in his garden was Toroni, but I only caught sight of his back as he was running away; his face was concealed by a high collar, and his hat tilted over his eyes. I watched you on deck this morning, it was blowing hard; your hat blew off and you ran after it. I saw your back and recognized at once the motion of your arms and your gentle tiptoeing. No, don't interrupt me ... the identification was conclusive. What should you say if I had you arrested on the spot and your four trunks containing 'antiques,' searched? Would you describe the two wooden dolls also as antique curios?"

Ferail had not moved, but he continued to stroke his beard.

"Unfortunately, I must again repeat that I don't understand you," he answered; "your conversation is very odd but rather interesting. I am Ricardo Ferail, born at Salonika, but an American citizen for the last ten years. I have visited your beautiful country in search of antiques, and can produce papers bearing me out."

"Of that I have not the least doubt," replied Wallion. "I am sure you protected yourself perfectly well."

"Now, supposing I were that Toroni," the Greek resumed, "should I be so careless as to have those dolls among my luggage? ... I can't tell ... but it seems to me that I should rather have sent them through the post to some address you would not know—you can't open every mailbag that leaves Sweden—or have hidden them somewhere after having found out their secret meaning. I might even have destroyed them. There are so many ways. The arresting of that Toroni you speak of would be a ticklish undertaking. Meanwhile the secret of the wooden dolls might be hopelessly lost, to you and your friends."

"You are a clever fellow," said Wallion. "That's why I want to come to an understanding or at least to make a bargain with you. I can arrest you now— and it entirely depends upon yourself whether I shall do so or not, for you have a shocking disregard for human life, Toroni, and you have already made an attempt to silence Elaine Robertson for good and all. Now as we shall be, if I mistake not, fellow travelers as far as Seattle, to begin with—for I am not going to lose sight of you—what say you to a truce during the voyage? I let you run to the end of your tether, and you stop molesting Elaine?"

"And then?"

"That will be a question between you and me." Ferail reflected for a few minutes.

"Do you mean that I shall be arrested the moment we arrive at Seattle?" he said.

"How long respite do you want?"

"Twenty-four hours."

Wallion lighted a cigar and attentively watched the Greek. "I shall shadow you," he said.

"If I were Toroni it might, perhaps, prove dangerous," he remarked.

"I am not concerned about my own safety; you shall have your twenty-four hours, but I shall not be far off, I give you warning."

Ferail sank listlessly back in his corner and closed his eyes. "I accept the bargain," he said.

"All right," replied Wallion, rising. "Good evening, Mr. Ferail," and without so much as a nod or offering his hand he left the smoking-room. When he came down he found Tom sound asleep, and he wondered whether he should wake the young man to tell him what had happened.

"No, I won't," he thought. "Time enough when we get to Seattle ... That is where the struggle will begin."

That night Wallion enjoyed good, sound sleep, such as comes after hard work.

CHAPTER 11

A "WELCOME" GIFT AT SEATTLE

A few hours before the liner was due to run into New York harbor Doctor Corman approached the two Swedes, who were leaning against the railing.

"Allow me to make a suggestion," he said in an amicable tone. "We have before us a long journey by train right across America, and I suppose your destination, like our own, is still Seattle?"

"It may not be our final one," answered Wallion; "at any rate it is our nearest."

The doctor raised his hands as deprecating Wallion's ambiguous reply, and said: "Then let us form a little, exclusive friendly party and our journey will be the pleasanter, will it not? Elaine is nearly well again now, but for her sake we should agree to let all business matters rest until we arrive."

"Of course, we quite think so," replied Wallion. The suggestion met with unqualified approval from Tom, and he almost began to like the Doctor.

When the statue of the goddess of Liberty, and behind it the turrets of the sky-scrapers, became visible, the passengers emerged from their cabins one by one. Elaine and Madame Lorraine joined the men and the conversation became lively. Elaine, though still pale, was evidently on the way to recovery. Tom had to acknowledge that the prohibition which had bereft him of the sight of her for some days had really been a happy thought, and that, too, made him more favorably disposed towards the doctor. He could hardly take his eyes off her thoughtful, attractive face, and said:

"I trust your principles with regard to the journey by rail are less rigid than with regard to a voyage by boat."

"How so?" she asked.

"So that we may enjoy more of your company, I meant to say."

She smiled, but there was a look of anxiety in her eyes, which she steadily turned towards the land. Signals of all descriptions came from the ships, a heavy shower fell, the seagulls shrieked, and there was a stir in the air. Immediately before landing, Wallion came up to Tom and hurriedly whispered in his ear: "Stay here with them and lend a helping hand with our luggage at the Customs; I shall look you up later."

He hurried away and found the man answering to the name of Ricardo Ferail at the head of the big stairs. They had not exchanged a word since that memorable night in the smoke-room. Without any preliminaries Wallion said curtly:

"I intend to be near you when your luggage is examined; come along, it is time."

Ferail began to move without answering, and went down the steps, Wallion close at his heels. Twenty minutes later, the journalist was convinced that Ferail had not got the dolls with him, for the four enormous trunks contained a jumbled mass of curios and antique objects which seemed to have been scraped together without care or knowledge; but there were no well-known wooden images. Wallion looked at Ferail, who was watching the proceedings inert and silent.

"I am half-inclined to believe that you did send them through the post, Toroni," he said, in a low, sharp tone. "The other alternative you spoke of is less likely; ... you reckoned to arrive at the same time as the parcels ... and you must have an accomplice, a receiver ... at Seattle, or where?"

Ferail turned livid with anger, but he neither looked up nor spoke.

"You are silent? Now listen, Toroni, would it not be wiser to save yourself and the Government police a heap of trouble? Confess now and I will see to the rest."

Ferail' shot a glance of deadly hate right into Walloon's gray eyes.

"No!" He sputtered out the word as if it had been poison, turned and went away.

* * * *

The express, with its shining row of Pullman cars, stood ready to depart, and a babel of voices, hurrying steps and creaking barrows, filled the huge station hall. Tom looked anxiously about for Wallion, of whom he had not caught a glimpse since landing. At last he saw him coming along, lost in thought, and Tom, much relieved, called out:

"I thought you had quite disappeared. Where have you been? The ladies and the doctor are already on board waiting for you." He stopped abruptly, for at that moment he saw the Greek antiquary climb up into one of the last carriages. He saw, too, that Wallion was keeping a watchful eye on the man, and said: "What! he, too. Where is that despicable creature going?"

"We shall see," answered Wallion—who was not inclined to tell how he had shadowed Ferail through half New York; and that the man had neither spoken to any one or sent any messages—and he heaved a sigh of relief when he saw his taciturn enemy safely ensconced in the train. "Get in," he said to Tom; "I'll be there in a minute,"—and he hurried off to the telephone.

He rang up the Secret Service Division in New York; the next minute a well-known voice, expressing surprise, answered:

"Hallo! Wallion, how do you do? I've just heard that you came over in the Swedish liner.... What in the world are you doing here—in this town?"

The Chief of the secret police in New York was looked upon as one of the cleverest officials in that city. Wallion had made his personal acquaintance in connection with a big English case, and so could confidently reckon on a very friendly reception.

"I intend to ask you for a little assistance," he said; "I am on my way to Seattle on a very tiresome job. I shall, probably, be able to requisition official help before long, but just now there is an important link missing in the chain of evidence."

"All right, I understand ... What shape shall it take?"

"Can I have a clever, reliable man to meet me at the station at Seattle?"

"H—m, what has he got to do?"

"To shadow a certain person for twenty-four hours; after that I think we can have him arrested."

"H—m, sounds promising. I'll supply your man. Tell me by what train you are leaving. Oh, indeed ... well, it shall be done, and say, Wallion, on your way back come and see me and have a smoke."

"Thanks," replied Wallion, laughing. He rushed back to the train, which was just about to move, entered the compartment into which he had seen Ferail disappear, and finding his man there engrossed in a paper and seemingly regardless of the outer world, went quietly to his own compartment and joined his party.

Tom was engaged in animated conversation with Madame Lorraine, and had even succeeded in bringing a smile to Elaine's lips. The long train journey once begun, a feeling of relief seemed to have come over all of them. For several days there would be no change; one would have a little breathing time and could, for the present, forget what the future might have in store. But Wallion's thoughts were with the pale, silent man sitting in the same train not twenty yards away, huddled up in a corner, waiting ... planning ... what?

The sociable relations suggested by Doctor Corman were outwardly maintained throughout the long railway journey across America; one cannot always vouch for what will happen nowadays on a journey by train, notwithstanding its amenities, its comforts, and almost uninterrupted contact with the outside world.

It would be an exaggeration to assert that all went smoothly and harmoniously, however. Doctor Corman's frigid politeness hardly glossed over his frequent sarcasms, and his whole bearing showed plainly that he considered the society of the two Swedes tolerable but absolutely uninteresting. Madame Lorraine had fits of silent abstraction, and Wallion, who noticed everything, used sometimes to wonder what she was thinking about. On several occasions, having noticed that she seemed to look upon her brother with contempt, he said to himself: "What does she know? ... and what does she expect? ... A silent woman is an incomprehensible anomaly even to her friends ... We are certainly a heterogeneous party."

In the meantime Wallion noticed with some measure of gratification that Tom and Elaine got on extremely well together. There were two, at least, who were not up in arms against each other, quite the reverse; in fact, day by day Tom's devotion became more marked, and Elaine's eyes shone with newly-awakened interest.

But Wallion had other things to think about. Hour after hour, as the train sped over the mountain and plain, he watched the man who posed as Ferail; and though they never spoke, each was well aware of the proximity of the other. Ferail remained perfectly silent; he never appeared in the smoking compartment nor on the standing platform to see the view.

On the day fixed for the arrival of the train at Seattle a telegram was put into Wallion's hands; it ran: "McTuft, will meet the train at Seattle. He is clever and discreet." He rubbed his hands, for he had been anxiously expecting some such communication, and at once despatched a long, detailed wire to McTuft, whom he had never seen, but who was waiting for him.

With a creaking of brakes the train ran into the station of Seattle. Wallion and Tom stepped out on to the platform with as much elation as one goes to the theater with on an interesting "first night." But they had no time to exchange words, as Doctor Corman and his sister came up to them.

"Mr. Wallion," began the doctor with a smile which displayed nearly all his teeth, "we have reached our destination and I am at your service. When may I count upon your visit to my Home?"

"The sooner the better," replied Wallion.

"Nevertheless, it may, perhaps, not be quite convenient this afternoon; Elaine is my sister's guest in our villa, which is also the asylum, and settling in again always requires a certain amount of time. Then there is my assistant who looked after the Home during my absence and will, no doubt, want to confer with me. Can I send you a message later, naming an hour?"

Wallion cast a quizzical look at the doctor.

"Thanks," he said. "Murner and I are staying at the Pacific. I will wait there for your message." He bowed and proceeded along the platform as if he wanted to look after some luggage. As soon as he had mingled with the crowd he drew forth his handkerchief and mopped his brow, whereupon a tall, gaunt young man approached as if by command.

"I am McTuft, at your service, Mr. Wallion," he said, touching his hat.

Wallion looked at him closely. At first sight the young Seattle detective looked like an awkward, simple, red-haired country lad; but there was something in his light blue, gentle eyes and wide, mobile mouth, that inspired Wallion with entire satisfaction.

"That's all right, Mr. McTuft, we shall get on very well together. Your job can begin immediately ... Do you see that man over there who is just passing through the stile?"

"The one that looks like a cross between Belshazzar and Judas?" McTuft asked drily.

"Yes, that's the man ... He calls himself Ricardo Ferail, dealer in antiques; you must follow him like his shadow wherever he goes; notice with whom he gets into communication, and report every step he takes to me at the Pacific Hotel before ten this evening at latest."

"Suppose he should leave Seattle, what then?"

"Send me a wire, and go with him."

The next minute McTuft had joined the crowd, rushed through the stile and disappeared in the track of the antiquary. Wallion smiled and followed more leisurely. Outside he encountered Tom; they exchanged cool good-bys with Doctor Corman and the ladies, who were just getting into a motor. Ten paces away Ferail was opening the door of another car. Wallion was startled, for he thought he saw the Doctor and the Greek exchanging a significant though scarcely perceptible nod. The two motors drew out of the station yard; a third followed close upon the one in which Ferail sat. McTuft had begun his task.

Wallion waited a little and looked after them until they disappeared. Was it a fact that Ferail had given a sign to Doctor Corman? He bit his lip.

"Let us drive to the hotel," he said. "We must hold ourselves in readiness. Things may move more quickly than I thought," he said to himself.

"What things?" said Tom, taken aback. But he got no answer beyond an impatient "We shall see."

As it happened, Tom was not in the humor for conversation; he had become so accustomed to Elaine's society that the separation left a great blank; her sweet face and gentle voice occupied his thoughts to such an extent that he felt both happy and miserable. They had been so near each other during the journey, and how was it going to be now?

The afternoon merged into evening as Tom and his friend sat silently waiting in the hotel, each immersed in his own reflections.

"What are we waiting for?" inquired Tom, at last. "Why don't you do something?"

Wallion vouchsafed no answer; he kept looking at the clock; it was getting dark. At eight McTuft appeared.

"At last," exclaimed Wallion, rising from his chair. "Where is Ferail?"

"Shall I report at length or will you simply question me?" replied the young Scotsman, curtly but pleasantly. "This man, Ferail, was the very devil for giving me trouble. I shadowed him in a car and he did only two things worth mentioning. At 6:30 he telephoned to Director Edward A. Dixon."

"To whom, did you say?" burst out Wallion.

"To Director E. A. Dixon," repeated McTuft.

"Elaine Robertson's employer," Wallion whispered to Tom, who sat silent and dumb-founded. "All seems turning out well, as you see. Now what more?"

"Ferail inquired whether the 'goods' had come. The answer seemed to satisfy him."

"So the 'goods' have arrived," observed Wallion, whose eyes glowed triumphantly, "and then?"

"Then our man drove to his lodgings at 39 Church Street, and there he remained; I put on a man to watch whilst I am here, but first I drove to Headquarters to get a few particulars, as you see." He gave Wallion a paper from which he read aloud:

> "RICARDO FERAIL. Greek. Age 42.—Professes to be a dealer in antiques, but has no real profession or business; otherwise known as a professional gambler. Never convicted. Nicknamed 'Silent Ferail.' Is not an American citizen. Has been living for the last eight months at 39 Church Street.

> "EDWARD ATTISWOOD DIXON. Born in New York 1859. Well-known business man in Seattle. Supposed to be insolvent. The dispute with the Insurance Company about the the summer hotel burnt recently was decided in his favor. The sum paid by the Insurance Company saved him from bankruptcy. Owns five hotels and a wharf on the coast. Has extensive import connections."

Wallion gave McTuft a hearty slap on the back.

"Good," he said. "You know your business. Now what about the other matter in hand to which I referred in my telegram."

McTuft shook his head. "I have not been able to find out anything at all about King Solomon. There is no record of any King Solomon mines, and nothing about a catastrophe in Alaska which might fit in with your theories, in the Seattle papers of 1902. On the other hand we've got Doctor Corman," McTuft continued undisturbed, in true reporter fashion. "Towards the end of the nineties he was accused of poisoning at Chicago; his wife died of arsenic poisoning. He was pronounced 'Not Guilty.' At present he is Dixon's most intimate friend and lives, in part, at his expense."

Both Wallion and Tom stared in amazement at the detective, who retailed his news with no more emotion than if he had been talking about the weather.

"Well, and what about the sister?" inquired Wallion when McTuft had finished.

"There's nothing of any importance about her," said McTuft.

"And what about Corman's asylum?"

"It's quite correct that he is a medico," the Scotsman said, shrugging his shoulders. "Want to know anything more? Well then, I'll go back to 39 Church Street."

He went, and for some minutes Wallion stood as if dead to all his surroundings; his nostrils quivered and his lips were pressed hard together. All at once he said:

"I take less interest in Doctor Corman's past than in the fact of his connection with Dixon, the kindly employer who was so much interested in Elaine Robertson's history ... the chain is complete now. Scarcely had Ferail set foot in Seattle when he inquired about certain 'goods' at Dixon's, the 'goods' being the two stolen dolls, and it was to Dixon he had sent them from Stockholm. Again, I am perfectly sure now that Corman and Ferail exchanged signals at the station. They are old acquaintances, but they kept it secret from us. Dixon, Corman and Ferail, there we have our enemies."

"But who, then, is this fellow Ferail?" asked Tom.

"Haven't you already guessed? He is Toroni, of course."

A waiter came up just then.

"A gentleman is here asking for Mr. Wallion; his name is Henry Morris."

"Show him in."

A pale, short-sighted man in black came forward, and after an awkward bow said: "I am Doctor Corman's assistant. The doctor sends his compliments and he hopes to see you, gentlemen, at the asylum at 11 tomorrow morning."

"Thanks, are you going back there?"

"No, I gave up my post today and am leaving for Portland by the night train. I offered to leave his message on my way."

"Is that so?" said Wallion, very deliberately. "Does Doctor Corman intend to look after his patients alone then?"

"He has only one."

Wallion nodded, it was just what he had expected. He accompanied Morris to the door and said:

"Nice place, Portland, are you going to set up in practice there?"

"No, I am going to be assistant surgeon at the hospital," replied Morris, and with a stiff inclination of the head he left the hotel.

Tom, who all this time had been on tenterhooks, rushed at Wallion and seized his arm.

"What is the meaning of it all?" he said. "You say that Ferail is Toroni and Corman's friend; why didn't you have him put in gaol?"

"Because I want to find out first where those wooden dolls have got to," replied Wallion calmly, "but I am rather beginning to fear that I gave him too long a respite." After a pause he added: "Tom, we shall have to..."

Again there was an interruption; a waiter appeared with a biggish parcel done up in blue paper. "For Mr. Wallion," he announced.

"Hallo, what next? Who left this?"

"A little chap, who ran away immediately, sir."

Wallion made a sign to the man to leave the room, and proceeded to undo the parcel. It contained five wooden dolls, exact facsimiles of those with which they were already only too well acquainted. Wallion picked up a card on which was written, in a fine female hand:

"If you want to hear more about these dolls come to the West Seattle railway station one hour after midnight."

"What on earth is it?" said Tom, rather scared.

"'Welcome to Seattle,'" said Wallion, bursting into a fit of grim merriment. "A few playthings to amuse us whilst we are waiting."

He examined the figures minutely one by one. Under the foot of each he found a number; these were respectively: 1, 3, 7, 9 and 11.

"Uneven numbers only," he grunted; "with the one we took out of the girl's satchel the series from one to eleven would be complete. Yes, that is rather puzzling; an unknown giver," he said with a sardonic smile, looking at the card once more. "H—m, West Seattle station at one o'clock in the morning." He tore the card to pieces. "No," he said in a hard voice, "that trap is not good enough. Put those images into a bag, Tom ... we'll have another look at them later on."

He paced up and down the room for a time, deep in thought; then he spoke: "They want to keep us out of the way till tomorrow, that is why they want us to keep the appointment tonight; Tom, I shall require your assistance; I mean to pay a little surprise visit to the doctor and his friends tonight."

CHAPTER 12

WILLIAM ROBERTSON

Doctor Corman's villa and private asylum lay just outside and to the north of the town. At ten P.M. Wallion and his friends got out of a taxi which drew up a hundred yards from the heavy iron gates of the villa and, as they anticipated a long, tedious wait, they sent the chauffeur home. Their object was to find out who was there and to interfere in case of need only.

"Remember that William Robertson is there," was Wallion's cautious remark; "we must be careful not to bring things to a premature crisis."

They passed by the gates and climbed over a wall protected by shady trees. The night was dark, cloudy, and very still; there seemed no other houses near. They landed in what appeared to be badly kept marshy ground. The villa lay immediately before them, a pretentious, modern stone building on two floors, with a loggia giving on to the grounds, and a spacious lawn in front whence a short drive led to the gates. A faint light burning in a room over the loggia revealed that there were iron bars to the window. With the exception of this feeble illumination there was nothing on this side of the house to indicate that it was inhabited; but Wallion made a noiseless investigation of the other side and discovered lights in two windows on the second floor. These had no bars—merely thick curtains.

"I am thinking of climbing up to that barred window," he whispered, when he again joined Tom, "wait for me here." And before Tom could expostulate Wallion had climbed on to the roof of the loggia, and disappeared from sight. For a few minutes he lay at full length on the zinc roof and listened intently; hearing nothing he stealthily crept up to the window and looked in.

What he saw was nothing less than a whitewashed cell with a single lamp suspended from the ceiling; the furniture consisted of a strong wooden stool, a wooden table, and a wooden bedstead securely fixed to the wall. A man lay on the bed. Wallion recognized him at once, thanks to the photograph in Elaine's locket; the neglected white hair, the emaciated features and the feverish bright eyes had left a deep impression on his mind. He was William Robertson. He lay motionless on his back, his hands clasped under his head. Wallion looked long and pityingly at him through the thick glass. There was nothing in William Robertson's expression to indicate madness;

his face wore a look of apathy and calm resignation. The poor man, a prisoner rather than a patient, the object of their search—would he be able to answer the questions put to him? Wallion looked towards the door. It was locked, no doubt. How dark and dismal the house must be! ... Why was Elaine not with her father? He stopped to think, and then crept along the roof as far as the other windows which had no bars, but were now in complete darkness; he gently tried one of them which did not appear to be fastened; it yielded without any noise and he stepped in. The room in which he found himself was small and led into a dimly-lighted passage; he thought he could detect a faint odor of tobacco. Finally, hearing nothing, he crossed the room and looked out into the passage. A lamp hung from the ceiling at the farther end, and he perceived the balustrade of a staircase, and several doors—all shut. He walked along a red carpet to the end of the corridor, and there found that one of the doors, which seemed to be more massive than the rest, was padlocked, but the key was in the lock. Wallion's bump of topography told him that this must be the door of the cell he had seen through the window. Without another moment's hesitation he turned the key and went in. The man on the bed slowly raised himself, but Wallion quickly closed the door and laid a finger on his lips.

"All right, Mr. Robertson," he said with a smile, "don't be alarmed. My name is Wallion. I have come from Sweden and bring a message from Christian Dreyel."

William Robertson looked steadily at him, not with fear, but with an almost childlike curiosity.

"You are welcome, Mr. Wallion," he answered in a voice the strength of which had been sapped long ago, "don't be afraid that I shall make a noise. My daughter has told me all about you and your friend." In a low and hopeless tone he added, "But you have come too late."

"Too late? ... Not a bit of it.... It is never too late for anything," said Wallion soothingly, sitting down on the edge of the bed. "Your daughter is here safe and sound, and we are going to help you; but time flies, and you must tell me everything quickly, precisely and without reserve. My friend Murner is waiting outside, and no one has the remotest idea that I am here with you."

Robertson wrinkled his brow in a painful effort to understand.

"If they did know," he whispered, "you would not get out of here alive. I am in a prison; they insist on taking me for a madman. I am not mad—but expect I soon shall be. Oh, if you only knew what I have to go through. Their prisoner ... their prisoner..." and he laid his hand on Wallion's coat sleeve.

"But your daughter?"

"They have deceived my daughter."

Wallion saw a spark of fire in the dim eyes as Robertson leant over nearer to him, and deep in those hollow orbs there glowed a soul driven to the utmost border of reason, appealing for help. Wallion was seized with inexpressible compassion, and by way of encouragement took the cold, weak hands into his own warm ones.

"Try to set your mind at rest," he said. "But tell me: am I to understand that your daughter is not aware of the treatment Doctor Corman metes out to you?"

"Doctor Corman is cunning," whispered Robertson. "He enticed me here at first when I was sick ... Yes, when I was cast down and ill he took me up in a kind, friendly way; I was put into a pretty little room on the other side of the corridor, a sweet little room with no bars." ... Here he lost himself ... "without bars," he repeated.

"Yes, I see," said Wallion, "so he was kind to you for a time ... but one day you got to know that he was a friend of Toroni's, did you not?"

Robertson looked up in fear.

"Do you really know everything?" he gasped. "That was it; Toroni was alive and prying into the secret. Toroni was Doctor Corman's friend, but though the Doctor was sly and deceitful, I saw through him and his many questions at last; then they moved me in here. But listen how artful he was. When Elaine came to see me I had to receive her in that pretty little room as if it were still mine, and behind a curtain Toroni watched, revolver in hand, ready to shoot me, if I revealed the least thing. Can you imagine such a thing?" he burst out, raising his clasped hands. "And he would have killed us both had I ventured to say a word."

"Anyhow, you managed secretly to persuade your daughter to undertake the voyage to Sweden."

"Who knows whether that also did not leak out? I believe it did," Robertson answered languidly. "I had sent off the dolls before I came here. They probably decoyed me here so that they might find out their whereabouts. I am inclined to think so...."

Wallion nodded: "There's not the least doubt of that; Toroni and his accomplices went about their work thoroughly. Do you think your daughter has the least inkling of the plight you are in?"

"No, but I believe she begins to think the Doctor's diagnosis of my case is wrong," replied Robertson in an unusually natural and deliberate voice. "She told me last night that I am going to be taken away from here, and that everything would be made clear...."

"Oh, there she is right enough," said Wallion, "but a lot of things have to be done before then. You must place full confidence in me, Mr. Robertson, and tell me all," he bent forward. "Tell me what is the mystery about King Solomon?"

William Robertson raised his hand to his forehead as if to disperse the mist of years; it shook and the fire in his eyes died down once more.

"Oh, of course, I will tell you," he said half absently, "the time has come that I should tell you, perhaps, though you had better read it..." he roused himself. "I've written it all down—the account of King Solomon, you shall read it...."

All at once he looked with more intelligence at Wallion.

"I wrote it all down when I was in that room on the other side of the corridor. It is the first door on the left; there you'll find the document as well as a list of the twelve."

"What twelve?" broke in Wallion excitedly.

"Well, the list of the twelve who were the rightful owners."

Wallion was about to speak, but Robertson resumed with feverish haste:

"Go in there, open the window and feel along the molding on the further side; that is where the papers are, wrapped up in a piece of oilcloth. I hid them there."

Greatly surprised, Wallion smiled.

"A very good hiding place, too," he said reflectively. "Things seem quiet enough in the house," he continued, "and those documents I certainly must have...." He lifted a warning finger. "A motor is coming up the drive."

The hum of a motor, and the grinding of wheels on the gravel could be heard distinctly on the other side of the house. Wallion turned to Robertson and said:

"Stay here, and be calm; I'll come back soon, if I can; anyhow, you will be free tomorrow at the latest. Trust me."

He gave a parting nod to the poor man, who looked wistfully after him, and went out. There was no one in the corridor and he locked the door so as not to raise a sudden alarm. On the farther side of the house he heard a door open and stopped to listen. There was no other sound, but he thought he heard the murmur of voices behind one of the doors a long way down. He frowned and hurriedly transferred his Browning from an inner to an outer pocket; then he made his way into the "sweet, little room" which had been the unfortunate man's first resting place in the asylum. It was simple but bright with flowers on the table, most likely put there by Elaine.

But Wallion had no time to waste on details. Without striking a light he opened the window, stepped out, and with his hands groped along the molding above his head. Immediately below he noticed the shining black hood of a motor, with shaded lamps and faintly humming engine, but there was no one to be seen in the drive. Wallion observed these facts mechanically, for his hands had already grasped a roll of something which had been hidden in the molding of the wall above the window. He got down satisfied and elated, and closed the casement again. "At last," he said to himself, "at last the key to the mystery is in my hands." He took a few steps into the room, but suddenly stopped short, every nerve in his body whispered "Danger," and his hands sought his pocket. The electric light was switched on, and in the doorway stood Doctor Corman.

"I beg you to keep quiet," said the Doctor, with his usual cold, well-trained voice, "and hands up, if you please." A revolver gleamed in his hand—and Wallion obeyed.

"Delighted to meet you here *en famille*, Doctor," he said smiling, "I know now how keenly I appreciated your worth during our railway journey together."

"What business brings you here?" asked the Doctor curtly.

"Did you think I was going to play with dolls like a good boy, and go to the station at West Seattle at one o'clock in the morning?" said Wallion. "No, the card you made Madame Lorraine write did not lure me, and I hadn't patience enough to wait until eleven o'clock tomorrow; that's what has brought me here."

"And you preferred to sneak in like a thief?"

"You are very particular ... I got in where I could."

"You will be received accordingly. Be good enough to keep still; our explanation will be short but to the point."

Wallion's eyes wandered to the left, where he suspected a door concealed behind a curtain.

"As you please," he said, "but I think our friend Ferail had better show himself too. Aha, he is hesitating, perhaps he would rather be addressed by another name. Now, then, come along, No. 13 Toroni."

The curtain was drawn aside and Ferail appeared in the light. He also had a revolver in his hand.

CHAPTER 13

FERAIL MAKES A PROPOSAL

"Good evening," said Wallion, in an amicable tone. "You are right in making the most of the fleeting moments; your twenty-four hours' respite has not quite run out yet."

The Doctor was as imperturbably cool as ever but Ferail's countenance had altered indeed. His upper lip was drawn up above the gums, his eyes were burning, and the skin of his distorted, repulsive face had turned to a greenish pallor, as if his choler were choking him.

"I can do without your respite, Wallion," he said. "Did you think I could not shake off that simpleton McTuft? You had better get some other man in his place, for he is no good. Why don't you have me arrested now, eh?"

"Have you arrested? Certainly not ... your conversation is so exceedingly pleasant...."

"Enough of that," interrupted Doctor Corman, "Ferail, get that roll our visitor is holding in his hand. He has had better luck than we, he has found Robertson's notes.... I am sorry, Mr. Wallion, but they don't belong to you. Take them, Ferail."

The Greek did so, and went with great thoroughness through the pockets of his victim, though he took nothing except the Browning, which he threw on the sideboard.

Steps became audible in the corridor, and a stout but active-looking man in a well-fitting chauffeur's uniform, walked in.

"What is all this delay about?" he said sharply. "Haven't you settled it yet, boys? Who the deuce is that man there?" he added, staring at Wallion who, being now without a weapon, stood with his arms at his side and his hands in his pockets, leaning against a chair.

"He is one of those Swedes," answered Corman. "We caught him in the act of stealing some papers of Robertson's."

"My name is Maurice Wallion, at your service," said the journalist detective, with a mocking bow, "I presume I am addressing Mr. Edward Attiswood Dixon?" The name rolled glibly off his tongue.

He had made a shrewd guess at the owner of the black motor, and he examined him with undisguised curiosity. In spite of his corpulence the man moved with well-trained ease and self-possession; his face was ruddy, and he was bald with the exception of a little gray fringe at the back of his head. His features were full and coarse—a face like that of Nero up-to-date, made in America.

Wallion was not disappointed, he had pictured Elaine's employer something like this.

Dixon slowly took off his driving gloves and let his eyes, which were entirely devoid of expression, rest on the "Problem-Solver."

"Well, Mr. Wallion," he said, "you seem to be in rather a fix just now. Pray, are you always so imprudent?"

"Of course, life would be so monotonous otherwise."

Dixon showed no sign of having heard this remark. He took the roll out of Ferail's hand and stuffed it into one of his inner pockets.

"I am going to look after this," he observed in a business-like voice. "We are in a hurry, the road is clear and I've got the two dolls in the car. What are you going to do with him, Doctor?" he asked, with a movement of his hand in the direction of Wallion.

"Allow me to make a proposal," said Ferail, taking a step forward. His peculiar short breathing made every one look at him.

"Well, what is it?" asked Dixon abruptly.

Ferail's face twitched, he looked like one possessed, his right hand wandered to his waistcoat and he drew forth a long, straight, thin knife…. "This is what I wished to propose," he said.

The knife was as bright as though it had been polished with the utmost care, and Wallion had not the least doubt that, barely two yards away, his eyes beheld the weapon which had slain Victor Dreyel, all but killed Christian and severely wounded Elaine. Ferail had put his revolver back in his pocket, he seemed to despise any weapon other than his shining blade, and he no longer fixed his eyes on Wallion's face but came closer up to him….

"Ferail," said the Doctor.

The Greek stood still.

"Your methods are not ours," resumed Corman. "Put that thing away."

Ferail lowered his eyes and stood for a time with head bowed low, then silently put the knife away.

"That is well," said Wallion, "but I shall not forget your gentle proposal, Ferail."

The Doctor and his friend exchanged a few inaudible words, whereupon Dixon said in a loud voice: "The simplest way will be to shut him up in that little room down there."

Doctor Corman nodded assent, and turning to Wallion: "Come along," he said, in a tone of command. "Go down the stairs in front of me, and take my word for it that I will shoot you down without the slightest compunction at the very first attempt of escape."

"Thanks, your attitude with regard to the fifth commandment is original, very," replied Wallion, and laughed as he made his way past his adversaries. In the corridor he stopped to light a cigar, and then went quickly down the stairs.

The Doctor threw open a door on the right, and with a sardonic smile motioned to Wallion to go in. Wallion, knowing that resistance would prove as fatal as suicide, resigned himself with apparent submission to the inevitable, and obeyed. The door closed upon him with a mighty bang.

He was left to himself in a cell even smaller than the one occupied by Robertson, while the bars of its window were more massive. It was sparsely lighted by a lamp suspended from the ceiling, but far out of reach, and the window also was set a good yard beyond the thick bars inside. There was not a stick of furniture of any kind. Wallion tried the door; it was of solid oak, with a lock impossible to negotiate from the inside.

"A regular prison cell," growled Wallion. "I wonder for whom it was originally intended."

He tried to look out, but the darkness outside prevented him from seeing anything, and he could not extinguish the lamp. He hoped most sincerely that Tom Murner would return to town and give information to the police that he had mysteriously disappeared, but presently, with silent scorn for his weakness, he remembered that he had not given Tom any instructions in case of such a contingency.

He heard footsteps and voices, both within and without, and realized that his last hope was gone…. He heard Tom Murner's voice in the entrance hall. He could not catch his words distinctly, but he heard the Doctor reply, "Yes, he is here. Do come in, you are very welcome, Mr. Murner."

Tom's voice seemed to draw near and sounded somewhat suspicious.

"Can I speak to him at once?" he said.

"Yes, of course…. This way, please."

The steps came nearer and Tom asked from outside, "Is Wallion here?"

"Yes, here he is, you need only walk in."

The door of the cell was opened, Tom was roughly pushed in, then it was slammed to again and sounds of loud, derisive laughter came from the hall. Tom picked himself up half-dazed. "You, too?" he said, lamely. Wallion made a wry face—he no longer felt any inclination to smile—and merely said: "As you see."

A dazzling light passed the window; the lamps of the motor car were being lighted ... Sounds in the distance indicated that it had started.

CHAPTER 14

1ELAINE'S SECOND DISAPPEARANCE

Wallion looked thoughtfully at the lamp. Then he took out his clasp knife, and with unerring aim, hurled it at the globe, which fell to the ground in countless pieces, and left the room pitch dark.

"What in the world did you do that for?" cried Tom.

"That I might look out," said Wallion, leaning against the window-bars, and gazing eagerly out into the night. The lights of the car below came round a turn of the drive and a black mass could be seen making its way towards the gate. Both men caught a glimpse of Elaine's head in the car before it was lost in the darkness. Tom nearly yelled:

"Oh, the wretches, they are taking her away."

"She is going with them of her own free will," said Wallion wearily. "Be quiet and let me think."

He sat down and crossed his legs, leaning against the wall, with closed eyes. After a time he began to relate all that had happened since he had got into the house.

"So you will understand that she has not the slightest idea of what goes on here, and that, in a way, makes her position more difficult," he concluded. "There is a possibility of their wanting to keep her as a sort of hostage, for she can scarcely have any further information to give them...." Here he stopped in order to think a little, "I wish I could have saved Robertson's notes," he continued, "then we might, perhaps, know where they are going now."

His cool, deliberate tone irritated Tom.

"I consider we have behaved like consummate idiots," he burst out.

"Yes, I have especially," Wallion drily confessed. There was something in his voice which filled Tom with self-reproach.

"Forgive me," he said, "I am almost beside myself."

Wallion pressed his hand in the dark.

"I am thinking about those dolls," he volunteered. "What Robertson said about a list of twelve who were the real owners, taken in conjunction with Victor Dreyel's words when he said the dolls were 'likenesses of the dead' which bring misfortune to the 'living,' has put a queer notion into my head. The figures were all numbered and we have seen sundry numbers up to twelve. Possibly these images really represent the 'genuine' proprietors, and there should be exactly twelve…. How does that strike you?"

"It sounds very likely," replied Tom.

"We have come across all the uneven numbers," Wallion went on, "in a way which rather seems to indicate that the uneven numbers are of no value. The figure that was stolen from Victor Dreyel bore the number 12 and the one his cousin had was marked 6. In what way, do you suppose, can the even numbers be of more value than the odd ones? The uneven numbers stood alone, but under No. 6 and No. 12 were some other numbers in addition, 29" and 33". Let us take the even numbers 2, 4, 6, 8, 10 and 12, and when we divide them into two groups we find on the last in each group the numbers 29" and 33". Now make a shot at something … guess!"

"No, I don't take that in," said Tom, "what are you aiming at?"

"Purely a supposition, just imaginary," replied Wallion. "Let us assume that in the year 1902 there were twelve men, proprietors of a gold-mine in Alaska, that the majority of these fell victims to some unexpected calamity; and that the few who survived returned, sorely disappointed, to civilized life. One of these, no doubt, was William Robertson, and two others, Victor and Christian Dreyel, cousins. Well then, if for some reason or other Robertson wished to record the longitude and latitude of the mine on the dolls, which bore even numbers, the degrees, minutes and seconds, you understand … one number on each figure … the seconds would fall to No. 6 and No. 12."

At last Tom seemed to comprehend his friend's theory.

"Yes, of course," he cried aloud, "and if the situation of the mine can be pretty accurately located the numbers referring to the seconds are indispensible. That was why Robertson sent Nos. 6 and 12 to the Dreyel cousins for safety, and why Ferail began his murderous work. Wallion, you have solved the mystery of King Solomon."

Wallion shook his head.

"No," he said. "I fancy I am pretty near it, though. Who is No. 13 Toroni? Where does he hail from? As I have represented things there are still various discrepancies. Can a mine disappear so entirely in the space of sixteen years? Could those fellows that drove away in Dixon's car have set to work in peace and quiet to exploit a stolen gold-mine? Why did not Robertson and the Dreyels go back again if it could be worked anew? No, King Solomon remains a riddle to us, my friend."

Tom relapsed into his former state of depression. What was the use of speculating when Elaine might be on the road to renewed dangers? He jumped up and began a wild attack on the door. "We must get out of this!" he said angrily.

Wallion, who had risen, walked to the window, turned round sharply, and said:

"Pull yourself together, man, in five minutes relief will come."

Tom, bewildered, muttered: "How?" Half hopeful, half in doubt.

"I rather think McTuft is standing by the gate," was Wallion's laconic reply as he fumbled for his knife, which he threw with all his might against the window between the bars; the panes broke with a crash which in the dead silence could be heard for a great distance, and almost immediately light footsteps sounded on the gravel outside.

"McTuft!" Wallion called out.

"Here I am," answered the Scotsman below. "Whatever are you doing there, Mr. Wallion?" he asked with apparent interest. "I thought the house was empty."

"We are shut up," replied Wallion briefly. "Creep in as best you can and open the door for us; I will knock so that you will know which door."

McTuft whistled softly and ran round to the entrance. After a seemingly endless time the door sprang open and they were free. McTuft could hardly restrain his curiosity.

In a few words Wallion told him what had happened, and fixing his eyes on the Scotsman, said:

"So you have lost Ferail?"

"Yes, the scoundrel made his way over the roof," said McTuft, visibly affected. "I did not know it was a habit of his.... Anyhow, I traced him here," he added.

"Well, by this time he is probably a good distance away from here, but I am not going to find fault with you on that account, McTuft, you helped so cleverly with the doors; did you come alone?"

"No, with my assistant, who is now waiting with the car a little way down the road."

"Splendid, call him up quick," said Wallion, as he ran upstairs. He unlocked the door of Robertson's cell, half afraid of what he might see within, but to his great relief he found the man in bed, lying on his back as before.

"Anybody been here?" he asked

"The Doctor looked in once without saying anything," replied Robertson, who sat up as soon as Wallion came in, more wide awake and expectant than he had seen him yet. "What has been going on? I heard steps and voices.... Where is my daughter?"

"You must take things quietly now," said Wallion kindly. "I can't explain matters just at present, but there is nothing to be alarmed about. Your daughter has left the house, but you will have news of her soon. You have done with your tormentors now, for good and all, and I shall put you under the care of a really trustworthy person."

At this point McTuft and his assistant, a young, pleasant-looking official named Johnstone, entered the room.

"There are two things you must do, Johnstone," was Wallion's greeting as he hurriedly scribbled a few lines on a card. "First of all you must take Mr. Robertson to the Pacific Hotel, give this card to the manager and see that he is properly looked after. Secondly, alarm the police. They must track the individuals whose names I have written down: Edward A. Dixon, Doctor Augustus N. Corman, Madame Lorraine and Ricardo Ferail, commonly called 'Toroni'; the last is guilty of murder, the others are accomplices."

Johnstone wrote down the names.

"They have only just driven away in Dixon's car, and under false pretenses induced Miss Elaine Robertson to accompany them," said Wallion more deliberately. "Her father, Mr. Robertson, need not be told, but he may give information respecting their motives and actions; got that down?"

"Yes," answered the young official with enthusiasm and, grinning at McTuft, observed: "'Hotel Dixon' is in for it this time. Just think of it!"

"That's good," said Wallion, "but you must provide yourselves with another car, the one that is here we shall want for ourselves; *au revoir*, Mr. Robertson, and don't you worry," he concluded, shaking hands heartily with the bewildered man, after which he hurried away.

It was past eleven, and darker than ever, when Wallion, Murner and McTuft ran down the drive to the gates. By the light of McTuft's pocket-lamp they could distinctly see the traces of Dixon's car on the damp road.

"They have taken a northerly direction, probably for the coast..." said McTuft.

They got into the car, and McTuft, who knew the country well, took the wheel; there was no need for any deliberation on the way, both Wallion and Tom knew exactly what to do. Dixon and his associates must be taken at any cost, in the least possible space of time, and sent to prison. Tom said nothing, but he was prepared. The picture of Elaine's sweet, innocent face among such repulsive surroundings as "Silent" Ferail's Assyrian profile, Doctor Corman's satanic features and mocking smile, and Dixon's Nero-like head, almost drove him frantic.

The motor flew along like an arrow and left Corman's dark, empty house far behind; the lights of Seattle disappeared from sight and all that lay before them was a desolate, white road, leading ... where?

CHAPTER 15

HOTEL "GOLDEN SNAKE"

A cool breeze was blowing from the sea, and far away in Puget Sound hoarse and peculiar signals, proceeding from an invisible steamer, filled the air. The last breath of wind, however, soon ceased, the atmosphere grew more oppressive and finally resolved itself into fog. The motor rushed on with careless speed, the impulsive, gruff Scotsman proving himself an ideal chauffeur. Fortunately, at that hour the road was almost deserted, and by the white light of the lamps the traces of Dixon's car, in double, unbroken lines, were plainly visible. All at once McTuft remarked:

"One would think they were making for the Canadian frontier."

"They won't get there," said Wallion, "it's much too far."

"Well, it is a good bit off, as you say," assented McTuft drily, "and I guess Johnstone has given the alarm by now."

They were getting near the water and, still following the track, they turned into a road which it seemed likely ran parallel with the shore in a northwesterly direction.

"Perhaps they intend going on board some vessel," suggested Tom uneasily.

"I was just thinking the same thing," Wallion answered.

At the same moment McTuft put on the brake, for a lad of about fifteen was coming from the opposite direction on a bicycle, and the Scotsman called out:

"Hallo, boy!"

"Boy yourself," retorted the lad, stopping. "Say, is there a motor-race on this evening, eh?"

"Have you met a black-covered car?"

"I have, and, my eye, it could run too; it dashed past me like a shot."

"How long since you saw it?"

"Ten minutes or so."

McTuft started the car and remarked: "They haven't got far ahead." Trees and bushes flew past and the travelers felt as if they were sitting still in the midst of a hurricane. Black pools of water were visible on the left, as they rushed past detached villas and groups of houses on the sea front. Now and then they met a car, which carefully turned aside to let them pass, and in a few seconds was left far in the rear.

But shortly afterwards, when the car was beginning to toil up a long ascent, almost parallel with the beach, McTuft again applied his brakes, and pulled up in front of a signboard which read:

GOLDEN SNAKE
SUMMER HOTEL

A gravel path led to a dark, high building which rose almost from the edge of the water. Near it was a tennis lawn, and further away a landing-stage for motorboats, a long line of bathing machines and several villas. McTuft pointed to the roadway. Evidently Dixon's car had pulled up for a few minutes by the side gate and then started again. A sleepy, uncouth individual in slippers and shirt sleeves was about to slink into the hotel by the kitchen entrance when a shout from McTuft stopped him.

"You, over there, come here!" The man turned and came slowly.

"Golden Snake Hotel! Curious name that for a summer hotel," said Wallion.

"It's named after this little bay which is called Golden Snake Bay," volunteered McTuft; "newly erected. Meant to make this into a fashionable watering-place, I guess, but I don't think it will attract many visitors—one of Dixon's unsuccessful speculations."

"What? Is this one of Dixon's Summer hotels?" asked Wallion in surprise. "If so..." He rose hurriedly and jumped out of the car.

By this time the man had come up, and Wallion inquired.

"Are you in Mr. Dixon's employ?"

"I am," said the man, and yawned.

"Your employer's car pulled up here a little while ago, didn't it?"

The man nodded.

"Well, what did he want? ... Now answer me quick or it will be the worse for you."

The man blinked his malicious, inquisitive eyes in the light, and scratched his head.

"Now then," said McTuft harshly ... "No nonsense."

"He had one of our chauffeurs called up from bed and took him," said the man reluctantly. "I can quite understand he must have been awfully tired driving the car himself all that time."

"Then he drove on again, I suppose; how long ago was that?"

"Five ... ten minutes, maybe."

Wallion looked closely at the man in slippers but remained dumb. McTuft gave vent to a war-whoop, he was madly impatient.

"Quick, get in again, Mr. Wallion, and let us be after them."

"No," said Wallion, "I stay here."

"What's that you say? ... You want to remain here? ... But what about the car?"

The Scotsman's red hair seemed to stand on end; he had taken off his cap and was staring at Wallion as at one who had suddenly taken leave of his senses.

"Can I speak to the landlord?" said Wallion, turning to the man, who stood there gaping.

"He has gone away, the hotel is closed for alterations."

"But it seems that there are chauffeurs?"

"Yes, we have the garage to let."

"We are wasting time," said McTuft in despair. Wallion looked at him and smiled.

"You are right, McTuft, I have changed my plans. Go after Dixon's car at once and stop it; perhaps Murner and I will come on later; no arguing ... be off." Wallion had spoken in a tone of command. The Scotsman straightened himself, bit his lip, and said, "All right."

Tom had only just time to get out before the car started and disappeared round the corner.

"What does all this mean?" asked Tom confusedly.

"It means," replied Wallion, "that McTuft, who is stubborn, is getting his own way, that the black car won't be running much further, and that the Golden Snake Hotel is much too interesting to be passed by..."

He pounced upon the sleepy man and caught him somewhat savagely by the arm.

"What is your job here?" he asked gruffly.

"Night watchman," came the sullen answer.

"Good," said Wallion, hustling the man in front of him along the gravel path towards the hotel.

"Then, of course, you can tell me what sort of people have been here recently and which of them have only just left." He pointed to the path where half obliterated marks of many feet were still to be seen.

The man's knees began to shake and he opened his mouth in dumb despair.

"Look here, my man, we are detectives, so you had better keep a civil tongue in your head. Well, you say that Dixon had a chauffeur in readiness here and that the black car went on again with that same chauffeur at the wheel?"

"Yes," stammered the man. Wallion seized and shook him like a rat.

"Now about Dixon himself, he got out here, didn't he? And his party as well; don't try to deny it," said Wallion, in a voice that nearly scared the man out of his wits. "They got out here; where are they now?"

The man lifted his hand and with trembling finger—he seemed unable to speak—pointed to the bay. Wallion pushed him away.

"To the beach," he said with a frown. "A boat! Aha, what is that? Over there?"

As soon as they passed the corner of the untenanted hotel they obtained an open view over the smooth water of the bay. Outside the breakwater lay a large pleasure yacht, painted white, with steam up.

"What sort of a boat is that?" asked Wallion sharply.

"That ... that is Mr. Dixon's steam yacht *Ariadne*," the man answered dejectedly.

Wallion looked at Tom. Both immediately grasped the situation. Wallion let go the man's arms and pointed to the house.

"Go in there and don't stick even the tip of your nose out of the door."

The man disappeared in the direction of the hotel, and he did not notice that he had lost his slippers on the way; the treatment he had received from Wallion had rather dazed him.

Wallion and Tom cast wistful eyes upon the pleasure yacht which lay proudly on the dark, gleaming water, smoke issuing from the yellow funnel ... She was evidently ready to start.

"I suppose they are on board already," said Wallion huskily. "Confound it all!"

He ran so fast towards the point that Tom could scarcely keep up with him. No one was near, but a prolonged whistle from the yacht came across the water, and Tom wondered whether it might be a signal to some other boat lying in the offing. Wallion had already climbed up the cliffs on the point, and as his silhouette became visible for a moment under the clear sky Tom fancied he saw him waving his hand. After much exertion Tom at last reached the top of the cliff; Wallion was nowhere to be seen, but when he leant over the rocks, a strange sight met his eyes.

From the foot of the cliff a boat, manned by four men, shot out into the water, but the men were sitting still with oars tilted, as if waiting for some one. Wallion came walking along the top some little distance away, heading straight towards the boat, and Tom felt by intuition that his friend had not noticed the skiff lying below. His voice froze on his lips—A short, nimble figure had thrown itself upon Wallion from behind, and both men rolled towards the edge of the cliff. There followed a smothered cry, a flash and the report of a shot; at the same time Wallion's body was jerked backwards and fell into the water with a splash. The short man scrambled hastily down the cliff and jumped into the boat, which immediately put out to sea. The beach was silent and deserted; the whole tragedy had not occupied five minutes and it left Tom cold, paralyzed and speechless. He ran like a maniac down to the place where his friend had disappeared.

CHAPTER 16

THE "ARIADNE"

The catastrophe had come like a thunderbolt, and though Tom did not doubt either his eyes or his ears, he could not help repeating to himself: "It can't be possible, it can't be true."

He had recognized Ferail's cat-like movements, had heard the shot and had seen Wallion fall into the water; he reached the fateful spot breathless and panting, and gazed into the dark, oily water which seemed to have no bottom. The cliffs were precipitous, but the water below was not very deep, though whatever was dropped into it was bound to be swept out to sea by the receding tide. Nothing was to be seen. Tom walked to and fro in the hope that Wallion might have swum ashore, but no trace of him could he discover. On the spot where the short struggle had taken place he picked up a spent Browning cartridge, that was all.

The boat with the rowers had gone also, and the outlines of the yacht were obscured by the rocks. The loneliness and silence fell upon Tom like a heavy weight; he threw himself down upon the ground, covered his face with his hands and groaned. Confused visions floated through his brain; he must seek help, give the alarm, inform the police ... Ten minutes went by without a sound save the splashing of the waves over the pebbles.

When he got up he shook as if from cold, his eyes were blood-shot, and he was conscious of one thing only, he must get away, he must ... He ran up the headland; the fog had become more dense and was driven in great masses from Eliot Bay, which appeared like a dark speck in the distance. The yacht was lying to about a hundred yards from the point, but its outlines were blurred and its lights looked like tiny glowworms. The sound of chains clanking and cogwheels moving came to the place where he stood.... They were weighing the anchors ... The *Ariadne* was evidently putting out to sea.

He rushed back to the landing-stage near the hotel—without further thought he had made up his mind. He was benumbed with pain and cold, and Ferail's repulsive features constantly rose up before him. How he longed to twist his fingers round the monster's throat! Wild, brutal impulses came over him like fits of ague; he saw red, sparks flew before his eyes ... Then there was Elaine, where had they taken her to, what was the fate in store for her? He set his teeth. Elaine must be saved at all costs.

Half-hidden under the landing-stage he discovered a small rowing boat; he jumped into it, cut the rope by which it was secured and laid hold of the oars.

The *Ariadne*'s propeller had begun to work, its rhythmical din seemed very near, and when he turned his head the green light on the starboard was only a few yards away; the yacht passed at half speed. Tom made a violent effort and the little boat lightly grazed the gleaming white side of the *Ariadne*. The lifeboat still swung from the davits and the end of a rope dangled within his reach; he seized it and hauled himself up; the little row-boat disappeared from under his feet and went dancing off on the cool waters. He climbed the rail and tumbled down on the deck, where he lay with beating heart, expecting a cry of alarm to be raised; but none came. The quarter-deck was deserted, but, immediately in front of him, under an awning, he could see the stairs leading down to the cabins. A table and three basket-chairs stood by their side; further on was a shelter and over all rose the captain's bridge, whence came the sound of voices, the only signs of life he could detect on board at that moment.

The yacht was larger than one would have supposed, seeing it from the land. It was clearly quite an up-to-date vessel of 500 tons, fitted with wireless, installed between the two lofty masts; under the awning an electric lamp was burning.

Tom was just going to pick himself up when two figures emerged from the stairs. Doctor Corman and Ferail were both smoking and had their coat collars turned up as a protection against the fog.

"Well, yes, I was rather taken aback when I caught sight of that devil of a Swede on the headland," said Ferail, as if he were resuming an interrupted conversation. "I thought he had seen the rowing boat, but I made the men conceal it under the rocks, and when Wallion came down he looked rather surprised.... I could have laughed if I had had time."

The doctor growled out something and Ferail continued, "Yes, with the knife, but he snatched it from me, and I had to shoot him instead; the bullet hit him between the ribs and he fell backwards into the water ... the water there is pretty deep, so we need not worry about him any more." A guttural sound which might have been interpreted as a laugh escaped Ferail's throat. "I told the men that I had only been settling up old scores with one of those 'black ones,' and they thought...."

Corman and Ferail went out of earshot.

Tom felt a wild desire to hurl himself upon the criminal, but he pulled himself together. They ascended the bridge and disappeared.

Tom lay completely stupefied. It was true then, incontrovertibly true, that Maurice Wallion was dead ... yet every fiber in his body seemed to repudiate the idea; he felt it unreasonable to believe that his strong, cool, stout-hearted friend, after Sherlock Holmes the cleverest expert in criminal cases, could in a single moment have been silenced for ever by this Greek imposter, this despicable monster. He buried his face in his hands ...

"I don't understand what is going on, but at any rate I must try to pull myself together ... because now I must do the work of two."

He knew he was dead tired. Gradually the yacht put on full steam, and the ripple of the water on the bows melted into a steady swish-swish. Like a sword through the fog shone the white rays of a searchlight.

Tom rose with a sigh of weariness; he felt stiff in every joint, and with a last remnant of clear intellect he said to himself: "I must bide my time.... If they discover me now I am lost."

He fixed his aching eyes upon the rocking life-boat. No, not that one; unsteadily he staggered over to the boat on the larboard, which was properly made fast and covered with a tarpaulin, under which he crept and lay at full length at the bottom; thinking that, for the present, at least, he would be safe there. No one suspected that he was on board, and no one would look for him there.

* * * *

At frequent intervals the siren on the yacht shrieked and was answered by signals from other vessels. The *Ariadne*, with full steam up, sped through the fog, which entirely prevented Tom from forming any idea of his bearings. Neither land nor water could be distinguished. He heard steps approaching and a deep voice which could be none other than Dixon's said:

"Well, Captain, we will go straight to Hurricane Island now. Think we can do it in three days and three nights? That is the time the last voyage took us, I remember."

"Oh yes, Mr. Dixon," replied another voice, clear, yet respectful and decisive. "We will do our best; the *Ariadne* is a good girl, and I suppose you are in a desperate hurry this time?"

"Never was in such a hurry in all my life before," said the owner of the yacht, in an amicable tone.

"H—m," said the captain, "we may have a storm, for at this time of year Hurricane Island deserves the name. If we don't, I promise you we shall be there by Thursday morning, Mr. Dixon."

"Not so bad," said Dixon. "Thursday morning then, eh?" He went down the stairs and the captain returned to the bridge.

"Hurricane Island," thought Tom, "whereever is Hurricane Island?" He made an effort to think over what he had heard, but the noise of the machin-

ery dulled his tired brain and with the raw, foggy air in his nostrils, he fell
into a heavy sleep.

PART III

HURRICANE ISLAND

CHAPTER 17

TORONI REASSUMES HIS RIGHT NAME

When Tom woke the sun was shining in between the tarpaulin and the rail of the boat, the air was mild—fanned by a feeble breeze—and the yacht rode easily.

Tom had to collect his scattered thoughts before he could remember where he was, and when he did get a clear idea of the situation a shudder ran through him. With great care he raised the tarpaulin and took a look round. The *Ariadne* seemed to be in the open sea, only from the starboard could he discern a faint blue outline of land; the waves rose and fell in gentle undulations which reflected the sun's rays, the fog was gone and the sky was almost cloudless. The fresh air revived him and he took a deep breath. Some distance off he saw two of the crew, barefoot, scrubbing and flushing the decks, and on the bridge he noticed the broad back of the captain. Tom looked at his watch. It was twenty minutes to one, and he had slept more than twelve hours!

The captain slowly turned round, and Tom again ducked down under the tarpaulin. He began to consider what he should do; but what could he do all alone? He clenched his hands until the knuckles grew white as he reviewed the terrible events of the previous night; but now he was better able to consider his position calmly, he rejected one after another, as impractical, his plans for revenge or escape. He did not even possess a revolver, nor did he know anything about the footing on which the captain and crew might stand with the three men who were his foes; perhaps they were all tarred with the same brush; anyhow, Dixon was the master or employer, and as Tom had no proofs, he was unarmed in a double sense. He spent an hour in fruitless brooding.

The name of Hurricane Island recurred to his mind. What sort of place might that be? There were islands all along the coast from Seattle to the Bering Sea, an archipelago hundreds of miles in extent, full of hiding-places and possibilities for lawless adventurers. The time mentioned for the duration of the voyage—three days and three nights—and his limited knowledge of geography gave him nothing to go upon, nor was he able to calculate the *Ariadne*'s speed, although it appeared very fair. He began to feel hungry;

that was a new trouble, difficult of solution. He remembered having read that lifeboats were always provided with fresh water and necessaries in case of sudden emergency, and he set about searching the boat surreptitiously, but found nothing.

"I shall have to wait till it is night, but something will have to be done then, for they shall not take me with my consent."

A stoical calm came over him; he understood that he could not do anything before darkness set in, and he lay down and shut his eyes in an endeavor to forget the cravings of his inner man.

Hours passed, the sun flitted from east to west, and the yacht kept on her course. Tom hoped the passengers would come on deck; the thought of Elaine, especially, filled him with longing; but no one came, and the deck remained deserted. The strip of land seen from the starboard had dwindled into blue mist, and all around nothing was to be seen but sea and sky; the setting sun dyed the horizon a dark, glowing red, and there thin banks of cloud stained it with a deeper hue and ever and again with fleeting gold.

Tom grew hot all over when he heard Doctor Corman's voice quite close to him, saying:

"It was lucky that we had the *Ariadne* to go to, otherwise we should not have been able to carry out our plans."

"You have always been a skeptic," Dixon answered. "The job is as good as finished, the plan worked like clock-work…. Now we have only to reap the reward of our labor."

They had evidently come up the gangway, for Tom not only smelt a whiff of tobacco but heard the creaking of basket-chairs and the clinking of glasses. Then there was a lull, and Torn could not resist the temptation to look over the edge of the boat.

Dixon, Corman and Ferail were comfortably installed in chairs round the table upon which bottles and glasses had been set. Dixon was rather red in the face; perhaps his dinner had been extra good, thought Tom, not without a touch of envy.

"Reward for our labor," exclaimed Dixon, with a laugh of greedy anticipation. "It was a difficult task to engineer, but with those two dolls in our hands all the rest is mere child's play."

"We shall, of course, be obliged to give up the *Ariadne*," said Corman. "We have left a pretty tangle behind us as it is, and, if I am not mistaken, that business of yours at Seattle will be thoroughly investigated."

Dixon again burst into a laugh. "I don't deny that I was rather too old to make a good man of business, but my last deal was certainly my best. Of course, the *Ariadne* must be sacrificed after Thursday next, as a description of her will be wired to every port and every boat today or tomorrow. So far, our own wireless has not received any little greeting; but don't you worry, it is sure to come."

"That's so, but our agreement is quite clear," put in Corman.

"To go shares and dissolve partnership at once?" laughed Dixon. "From Hurricane Island it is easy enough to get to Canada, and then I myself mean to go by the name of Christopher Cummings. What are you going to call yourself, Ferail?"

"From now till Thursday I insist on being known as Toroni," the Greek replied, in a muffled tone. "I am sick of the name of Ferail—it has a flavor of sour wine in my mouth; call me ... Toroni."

The two others looked at him in surprise, and yet as if they were used to his unaccountable outbursts of frantic rage and annoyance and could never be sure of his enigmatical temper. It was clear he inspired them with a sort of repulsive curiosity.

After a pause Dixon said, "As you like," and, raising his glass, he continued: "I propose a toast to Toroni, the name borne by a man who plotted and carried through one of the most brilliant transactions of the last ten years." His tone was a mixture of condescension and contempt.

They drank it, Toroni in gloomy silence; the doctor with a sharp, mocking laugh.

"In any case, my much esteemed friend Toroni," said Dixon, after momentary reflection, "it would be advisable to confine the use of your illustrious name to ourselves, or Elaine might take it into her head to have an attack of hysterics, and Captain Hawkins ... ha, ha, ha!" He concluded, overcome by a fit of hilarity: "It was a splendid idea of yours to pose as an Italian detective charged by the Government to investigate the secret affairs of the 'Black Hand'.... Detective Ferail, to whom I afforded my valuable assistance solely in the interests of the community. The captain and the crew are making themselves quite ill, racking their brains to find out what on earth you want to do on Hurricane Island. Well, old man, the comedy is too good to be spoilt.... Officially you are obliged to answer to the name of Ferail.... Good Heavens, man, we are about to pocket six million dollars in gold, pure gold, and you can be squeamish about a name!"

Dixon began to get excited, his voice grew louder and louder, and the doctor hurriedly seized his glass in order to put a stop to his half-crazy flow of words.

"A toast," said Corman, drily, "a toast to the six millions!"

His timely intervention saved the situation.

There was a bright light in Dixon's shifty and evil eyes as he raised his glass to drink the toast. "In gold, pure gold," he said.

Toroni did not look up nor did he touch his glass. Dixon fumbled with his hands in his great coat pockets, from which he produced two objects which he placed on the table; they were the two wooden dolls.

Tom recognized the one which had been in the possession of Victor Dreyel; the other had, undoubtedly, belonged to Christian Dreyel. The small figures glowed blood-red in the light of the setting sun. Tom gazed at them with a shudder, even the doctor seemed uncomfortable.

"Throw them overboard," he said abruptly; "they are no longer wanted."

"Throw them overboard?" retorted Dixon, reproachfully. "Our constant guardians, with whom Toroni had no end of trouble before he sent them to my place.... Never. I want to have them constantly before my eyes until the gold has seen the light of day, and then I shall return them to Robertson as a little souvenir."

Overheated with whisky and joyful anticipation, he unbuttoned his coat, took it off and threw it down upon a chair. "Poor old Robertson!" he soliloquized as he mixed himself another drink. "Things weren't very comfortable for him when he was your patient, you old compounder of poisons, you!"

Doctor Corman's face assumed an ashen hue, the eyes under his pince-nez flashed; but he restrained himself, and a painful silence ensued. It dawned upon Dixon that he had said too much, and he looked persistently at his cigar. At last Toroni lifted his tawny eyelids and said: "Talking of Robertson ... what do you intend to do with his daughter?"

That was a matter which had long occupied Tom's thoughts and now sent a shiver down his spine. Dixon became suddenly sober, and the doctor cast down his eyes without saying a word or moving a muscle. The silence seemed unending. At last Dixon said, impatiently, "Bah, Elaine? We brought her with us for otherwise she might have been a witness, but I..."

There was a rustling of silk on the stairs, and Madame Lorraine hurried up. She looked at the three men with undisguised loathing.

"Are you aware that the skylight above the saloon is open?" she asked.

"What do you mean?" inquired Corman, with some asperity. Each of them cast a quick glance at the skylight, which was indeed half-open.

"Only that I went into the saloon just now and found Elaine there." The three looked at one another.

"Think she heard?" the doctor asked.

"I can't say, but I heard every word you uttered ... distinctly."

"How did she look?"

"Much as usual," said Madame Lorraine, and left them.

Dixon had regained his self-control as if he had never tasted a drop of whisky; he took up the two wooden dolls and made his way to the stairs. At the first step he stopped, turned and gazed at them earnestly.

"Bah!" he said again. "If she had heard anything she would have screamed." Then he went down and the other two followed him. Tom breathed again; it was only now he remembered that he had been kneeling in the boat, with his head well over the edge, and that any one who chanced to look that way might easily have seen him. It was a miracle, indeed, that he had not been seen; but he had no time even to send a grateful thought to his guardian angel, for his mind was fully taken up with what he had just heard. Moreover, his attention was rivetted upon Dixon's overcoat, which had been left lying cm a chair, carelessly flung over the back of it, half-open, so that Tom could see a packet done up in oilcloth protruding from an inner pocket. He remembered what Wallion had told him about the scene at the asylum, and he realized that within five yards of him lay those precious papers of William Robertson's. His fingers itched, an irresistible desire seized him; he must have those papers and read them.

The sun had set, and twilight was beginning to melt into night; there was no one to be seen either on the bridge or on the upper deck ... nor was there any sound from the gangway. He got out of the boat noiselessly and walked warily towards the coat.

At the same instant a hand from the back of the cabin deck abstracted the roll from the coat pocket and disappeared.

CHAPTER 18

THE STORY OF "KING SOLOMON"

To say the least of it, Tom was stunned: the packet had been seized with such lightning rapidity that he had scarcely even seen the mysterious hand. At first, after his consternation at seeing the key to the secret disappear in such a way, just when he had felt it in his grasp, he could hardly collect his thoughts; it overwhelmed him.

Thoroughly exasperated and throwing prudence to the winds, he darted forward, intent on getting that packet back from this extraordinary thief. There was no one anywhere near the cabins; he closely examined all of them. The invisible thief was nowhere to be found. It was still light enough for him to be able to distinguish every detail on the upper deck; there was no hiding-place large enough for a cat, let alone a human being, and Tom experienced a sudden feeling of dread. "Whatever is it?" he thought. "Am I beginning to have delusions ... or to see visions?"

He heard Captain Hawkins' voice on the bridge, and he was fearful lest he should be discovered. Deadly white, he turned to port and climbed back into the boat. Just as he was about to lie down and pull the tarpaulin over him, he felt a strong arm pressing him down and a hand was laid over his mouth.

"Not a sound," said a low, deep voice, "it is I."

Tom's heart jumped into his mouth and then began to beat violently.

"Wallion?" he whispered, wild with delight and relief. "Oh, Maurice, I thought I should never hear your voice again," and he flung his arms round his friend's neck.

The Problem Solver was quite himself, but in the calm gray eyes it was easy to read how glad he was to see Tom.

"How in the world did you get here?" asked the latter, breathlessly. "Toroni was positive he had shot you, and I myself saw you..."

"Oh, no; things don't go so easily as that," answered Wallion. "When Toroni fired his shot I pretended to stagger, and fell backwards into the sea. I thought it was a good opportunity to let him think I was out of the reckoning. He is a splendid shot, though he is still more expert with the knife. So I did a dive, swam out a good distance, and when I came up again the row-boat was just starting. Then after swimming a little farther I let the boat pass, and followed it at a convenient distance as far as the yacht; and when you came up I was lying snugly hidden in the starboard boat. Had you chosen that retreat we should have been in one another's company from the first; still it is just as well you didn't, as for a little while I had to hide in a deck-cabin, whilst they turned out and cleaned the boat. I was afraid to wake you during the night, and by day it was, of course, impossible ... but how are you off for food?"

Tom put on a woeful expression and Wallion grinned.

"I've got a little something to begin with," he said, producing two long loaves, a tin of salmon, a piece of smoked sausage and two bottles of beer.

Tom must be excused for not doing more than casting a look of thanksgiving up to the sky by way of gratitude, as he fell upon the feast. With the aid of his knife Wallion skilfully opened the tin, uncorked the bottles without the least noise, and both set to with a voracious appetite.

"What do you think of the conversation among our three fellow travelers?" asked Wallion after a pause.

Tom, having appeased the most insistent pangs of hunger, said, with a touch of curiosity: "Then you heard it too?"

"Yes, I had made myself quite comfortable in the cabin; Dixon is a fine fellow, isn't he? You didn't seem to worry though; any one might have seen your head a thousand yards away...."

"You didn't trouble either," retorted Tom. "Of course, I was rather taken aback when the packet disappeared before my very eyes."

Wallion laughed and held it up.

"You see, in spite of that, the thing hasn't got lost," he said. He untied the string and unrolled the oilcloth, revealing several sheets of note-paper, covered with writing in a bold, clear hand.

"Let us take advantage of the daylight remaining and read William Robertson's notes whilst we are still undisturbed."

He smiled at Tom as he said: "Do you know I am beginning to feel quite nervous, for in another ten minutes the King Solomon secret and the purpose of the wooden dolls will be known to us? Such moments are well worth all the trouble engendered by one's vague speculations.... Just now I would not exchange these scraps of paper for the six millions Dixon talked about."

It almost looked as if he were going to postpone the reading.

"Quick, quick, I am dying to know..." ejaculated Tom.

"Well, we deserve it," said Wallion. Spreading out the documents, he bent over them and began to read. William Robertson's notes had the following introduction:

"Below will be found a true and, as far as possible, complete account of the destruction of the *King Solomon*, set down here that, in case of my death, it may prove of use to those who have an indisputable right to the precious contents of that ship.

"On August the fifteenth, 1902, the full-rigged American cutter, *King Solomon* started from Nome in Alaska for Seattle. The owners were Fraser, Hutchinson and Co., of Seattle, but this firm ceased to exist many years ago. On that voyage the vessel (500 tons) was commanded by Captain John P. Howell. Though not quite new, it was well-equipped; the crew consisted of eleven men only, because ten others had gone to the gold-fields. The insufficient number left was probably one of the causes of the disaster which overtook the ship later. There were thirteen passengers on board, twelve of whom were diggers, and a heap of gold as well. I, the undersigned, was also there, accompanied by Sandy McCormick, a Scotchman, and my two Swedish friends, Victor and Christian Dreyel; we four had been working a claim discovered by McCormick in the course of the summer, and each of us had gold on him to about the value of 200,000 dollars. We soon made acquaintance with the other passengers, of whom Craig Russel, a splendid man of the indomitable bandit type, nicknamed 'crazy or looney Russel' was the most important, seeing he had with him gold to the tune of 1,200,000 dollars. The other twelve were: Nicholas Sanderson, an elderly, quiet, unobtrusive Englishman; Aaron Payter; 'Colonel' Hyppolite Xerxes Symes, a well-educated, merry mulatto; Frederick O'Bryan, an Irishman; Jean Rameau, a Canadian; Phil Murray and Walter Randolph, two young Englishmen. The amount each one of these had on him in gold is recorded in the accompanying list.

"The thirteenth passenger, however, was a stranger unknown to any of us; he had no gold whatever, and his name was Toroni. No one knew where he hailed from, for he kept silent and aloof; but he was supposed to be an Italian. His melancholy demeanor seemed to presage ill-luck, and had a most depressing influence on all of us; so he was called 'No. 13 Toroni.'

"On board 'Looney Russel' was, so to say, boss. We, who with indescribable trouble and hard work, had wrested treasure from the desert, felt on our way back to civilized life like rich men; and naturally, we were constantly in a jovial frame of mind which did not always find vent in the choicest expressions.

"The gold, mostly well-washed nuggets, was in leather sacks, sealed, and packed in oak chests with iron bands. These chests or boxes—small, but too heavy for one man to lift—were fifteen in number, each being inscribed with a name. They were piled up in the saloon, and constant watch kept over them. Wild scenes took place in that saloon, in which gold to the amount of nearly six million dollars was stored.

"'Looney' Russel, by reason of his wealth and his tremendous physical strength, had constituted himself king of the revels; whisky flowed in streams, and gambling and drink were the order of the day. Russel, O'Brien, Rameau and Murray were the most inveterate gamblers, and hardly left the poker-table night or day. Toroni very soon chummed up with them; why I don't know, as he had never been looked upon with favor.

"Captain Howell tried to put a stop to these orgies, but failed. The second day of the voyage there was a great storm, the *King Solomon*, running before the wind, with top and foresail in ribbons. She had carried too much canvas as we were all anxious to get on ahead, but most of the desperadoes were too drunk to be of much use. Only the cousins Dreyel, the commander, and I, knew the state the crew were in, and foresaw, with great uneasiness, the impending catastrophe....

"On the morning of the third day, soon after four o'clock, the disaster overtook us. I heard shots in the saloon, and ran, only half awake, out of my cabin. Poker had been going on all night; Russel and Murray had lost fabulous sums to Toroni. Apparently Randolph had tried to persuade his friend Murray to leave off playing, but his well-meant interference had led to a general shindy.

"Then Russel suddenly found out that Toroni had cheated; and, mad drunk, drew his revolver and fired at Toroni, without hitting him. Captain Howell, who flung himself between them, had Toroni seized and locked up in his own cabin. But as I was leaving the saloon, Russel fired a second shot, and Captain Howell fell dead on the floor with a bullet through his head.

"Bellowing like a bull, the madman retreated to the companion ladder, firing at random as he went; Rameau got a bullet in his stomach, and died sitting in his chair. Murray, Randolph, and I drew our revolvers, but Russel darted up on deck, and when we went after him met us with a succession of shots from both his weapons at once. Murray fell, hit by two bullets, the mulatto, Symes, was wounded in the arm and Randolph in the head.

"The crew, already short-handed, were scared by these terrible events, and particularly by the death of their captain; the pilot left the wheel to escape the bullets, and *King Solomon* fell off her course. In less than a minute the ship presented her broadside to the waves and rolled so heavily that I thought we should go down at any moment. The first mate and two sailors went overboard while attempting to shorten sail and heave to; heavy seas broke over every part of the ship and stopped the fighting. 'Looney' Russel had disappeared in a wave and was seen no more.

"The second mate took over the command, but could not make himself heard. The ship drifted helplessly; the foremast went overboard, got caught in the tackle, and in a short time made a leak on the larboard side. The pumps were manned, but every one on board knew that *King Solomon* was doomed. Then some one shouted: 'Save the gold.' 'We'll thank God if we can save our lives,' the second mate replied.

"At 6 A.M. the life boats were launched in a sea the waves of which were mountain high; the long boat and the launch were dashed to pieces at once, but the quarter-boats were kept clear. Panic, however, reigned supreme—every one was madly intent on saving his own life. Six of the crew leapt into one of the quarter-boats with Sanderson, O'Bryan and McCormick, pushed off, and were swept away in the dark; that was the last I saw of them. I had no time to think, and I don't believe any one thought of the gold. Those of us still on board were making frantic efforts to lower the second quarter-boat. Then the mizzen mast broke, and a falling spar struck me; I fell unconscious down the cabin stairs, where I was washed into a corner with no one to help me. The rest of the ship's company, viz.: the second mate, the mulatto, Symes, Payter, Randolph, and the two Dreyels, left in the other quarter-boat, and the wreck drifted aimlessly in an easterly direction with me and six million dollars in gold on board.

"When I regained consciousness it was broad daylight, the storm had abated, and *King Solomon* floated low and deep on the big waves. I thought I was alone on board, but presently. I fancied I heard a faint knocking on the cabin door. It was Toroni, who had been locked in and forgotten! I let him out and we considered our position. There was one boat left on the ship,—the small gig,—but even that was badly damaged by the waves. It looked as if *King Solomon* were about to sink at any minute, and we set to work repairing the gig. There was food in plenty, but we did not allow ourselves time to eat. The fifteen boxes of gold still stood in the saloon, but we did not care to look at them, and whilst we were at work *King Solomon* still drifted eastward. I can't say whether it was on the second or third day after the shipwreck that we sighted land—those terrible days and nights are confused in my mind—but there *was* land at last, and *King Solomon* glided slowly in between two islands, divided by a broad channel. No houses, people or boats were to be seen, and the rocky shore did not look very inviting. *King Solomon*'s voyage was ended. The wreck began to sink rapidly in mid-channel; there was just time to push off the gig before the ship went down; and it was not till she had sunk that I realized what a loss was mine, that my hardly-won gold—and that of my mates—was lying at the bottom of the sea and that I was ruined. Fortunately the ship's instruments were in the boat; and with a vague thought that I might return some day and retrieve the gold from the deep, I fixed the place where *King Solomon* had sunk by seconds—for though the coast furnished infallible landmarks, the channel was more than a mile in breadth—and then ascertained that the wreck lay at a depth of about ten fathoms. Toroni was present but he had no knowledge of navigation and I am now aware that he made no copy of the bearings I fixed.

"Now as to the place: it lies among the islands that run along the coast to the most southerly part of Alaska. The largest of these is called 'Hurricane Island,' and is a rocky, deserted place, cut in two by the 'Black Valley,' which is covered in part by forest, and opposite the smaller 'Fir Island.' The channel between the islands is five miles long and one or two wide, with a depth varying from eight to twenty-five fathoms; there it was *King Solomon* went to the bottom. When I had thus located the wreck Toroni and I hoisted a sail and departed in a southerly direction. On the eighteenth day we were sighted by a Norwegian barque, bound for San Francisco.

"Of our condition at that time I will only say that the hardships we had gone through had affected our minds; that we were half-starved and feverish, and could not even give an account of what had happened. I was perfectly stunned by the catastrophe. We parted at San Francisco.

"I was told afterwards that the first quarterdeck boat had been lost, leaving no trace behind, but the second had reached land with Victor and Christian Dreyel as sole survivors. The papers did not get hold of the facts, and only one, a San Francisco paper, had a short notice to the effect that *King Solomon* had gone down with all hands on board. That notice was the cause of my wife's death. I was..."

Here Wallion turned a few leaves and remarked:
"We are already acquainted with William's illness and his fifteen years of crazy wandering; we will skip that."
They continued with the reading.

"The finding of my daughter was a turning-point for me; I began to make plans for the recovery of the gold which had lain so long at the bottom of the sea, but that required funds. I put myself in communication with the next of kin of the men who had perished on the *King Solomon*, and took steps to find their heirs. Then an unexpected thing happened. I came across Toroni in the street one day, under circumstances which clearly showed that he was spying upon me, and it was borne in upon me that some one wanted to steal the papers giving particulars of the place where the wreck lay. I was terribly worried. Partly to pass away the time I had carved wooden figures to represent myself and my eleven companions in misfortune, and had numbered them according to the accompanying list. I destroyed the notes referring to *King Solomon* after having engraved numbers denoting longitude and latitude on the feet of those dolls which bore even numbers—the latitude in degrees, minutes and seconds on dolls numbered 2, 4, and 6, and the longitude on those numbered 8, 10, and 12. As an additional measure of precaution I sent the two dolls which gave the seconds to the two Dreyel cousins. It was a well-conceived plan; for two days later—I don't know how—the rest of the dolls were stolen. This discovery aggravated my illness, and I felt that I did, indeed, require medical advice.

"But I fell from the frying-pan into the fire, and am now virtually a prisoner in Doctor Corman's villa. Edward Dixon is hoodwinking Elaine, and I cannot do anything to save myself. I am writing this in hopes that it may bring this diabolical plot to the notice of the authorities. Toroni is the prime mover in it; all these years, thoughts of the six millions must have been seething in his brain. I got to know that in 1904 he had made a secret attempt to get up the gold at Hurricane Island by himself. That was foolish; divers and modern appliances are required for such a purpose. Moreover, it is easier to find 'a needle in a bottle of hay' than to find a wreck ten fathoms below the surface, in a channel half a Swedish mile in length and over two miles in breadth. I cannot say whether he was preparing for a bolder stroke; at any rate, soon after, a decided obstacle came in the way.

"In 1913 a man, of the name of Compton, reported that he had discovered rich copper mines in the Black Valley on Hurricane Island; a company was formed, hundreds of workmen were sent out and operations on a large scale begun. The legend of the copper mine was exploded in 1917, and the islands were deserted. Now was Toroni's chance, he looked about for a capitalist and found ... Edward Attiswood Dixon, who appeared to make large deals and whose means were so ample that he no longer engaged in any regular business. He gladly agreed to Toroni's proposal; and for a ridiculously small sum acquired Hurricane Island and Fir Island, with the buildings left there by the former copper mine company. Officially he gave out that he meant to erect a repairing station for vessels trading between Alaska and the States; he did, in fact, build a breakwater with all modern improvements for sheltering ships, but that was only a blind to cover his search for the wreck of *King Solomon*, which was begun without delay. The search came to nothing; it only proved that my notes were indispensible. Then they got at Elaine, and through her I was enticed to leave my secluded quarters. Her engagement in Dixon's office and my incarceration at Doctor Corman's were only small items in their plans, but I was not going to give away the secret of *King Solomon*, if I could help it! I am hoping to escape, and as it may be necessary to get the two dolls back from the Dreyel cousins. I shall try to persuade Elaine to help me. If these papers should fall into the hands of honest people, I hope they will straightway send them to Headquarters.

"Seattle, July the third, 1918,

"William Robertson."

"LIST OF THE OWNERS OF THE GOLD."

1. William Robertson, only relative, one daughter, Elaine . . . 200,000 dollars
2. Nicholas Sanderson (drowned), probable relatives at West Hartlepool, England . . . 600,000 dollars
3. Craig Russel (drowned), family in Chicago, one brother in Melbourne . . . 1,200,000 dollars
4. Christian Dreyel, domiciled in Sweden, Captain Street, Borne . . . 200,000 dollars
5. Victor Dreyel, cousin of the above, domiciled in Sweden, 30 John Street, Stockholm . . . 200,000 dollars
6. Aaron Payter (died in boat, no relations . . . 800,000 dollars
7. Frederick O'Bryan (drowned), wife in Dublin, 142 Green Street . . . 800,000 dollars
8. Hippolyte Xerxes Byrnes (died in boat), probably mother and sisters in Louisiana . . . 500,000 dollars
9. Jean Rameau (shot on board), three sisters in Ontario . . . 200,000 dollars
10. Sandy McCormick (drowned), no relations . . . 200,000 dollars
11. Phil Murray (shot on board), parents in a village in Sussex, England . . . 600,000 dollars
12. Walter Randolph (died in boat), possibly relatives in Wales or Cornwall, England . . . 300,000 dollars

"Total . . . 5,800,000 dollars"

Wallion and Tom looked up from the last page at one another. It had grown so dark that they could hardly decipher the final lines.

"What do you think of that?" whispered Tom.

"It is beyond my most sanguine expectations," replied Wallion.

He rolled the papers up again in the oilcloth.

"What do you intend to do?" inquired his friend.

"I intend to replace the packet in Dixon's coat pocket. If he were to miss it and give the alarm, that would be an end to our liberty."

Wallion wriggled out of the boat and restored the packet to its place, after which he returned to his hiding-place; without a word he lay down on his back with hands clasped under his head. Tom, who thought his friend must be turning over in his mind the amazing story they had just read, did not venture to break the silence for a time. At last one of the thousand questions with which his brain was teeming could no longer be restrained.

"Maurice," he said, "do you think McTuft has any idea where we are?"

Receiving no answer, he bent down to look at his friend and repeat his question.

Maurice Wallion was sound asleep.

CHAPTER 19

WHERE THOMAS FALLS INTO THE HANDS OF THE PHILISTINES

Next morning there was a strong wind, and the yacht pitched a good deal; the violent motion woke Tom to find Wallion already awake. A shower of rain came down, but under the tarpaulin, though rather cramped, they were dry. Now that the mystery of the wooden dolls was solved, Wallion resumed his usual placid demeanor. They breakfasted on salmon, bread and sausage and then, in subdued tones, discussed the information gleaned from William Robertson's notes.

"It never occurred to me that *King Solomon* might be a wrecked vessel," remarked Wallion thoughtfully. "I wish I had known that three days ago; it rather alters the situation. Evidently our adversaries do not contemplate a long delay; they have brought divers, and all is clear at the so-called 'wharf.' Having located the spot only a few hours are required for hauling up the gold. I wonder..."

He laid his finger on his lips and his hand on Tom's arm; footsteps could be heard on deck.

"Thursday morning," said Doctor Corman irascibly, "that is rather late, Dixon."

"Rubbish! Why?" asked the owner of the yacht.

"Why? Because I am under no delusion about what we have left behind. Wallion is out of the reckoning" (here the latter pinched Tom's arm), "but don't forget McTuft, who was at Toroni's heels, and Wallion's Swedish friend, too, would not be idle either; it is quite possible that he was at the Golden Snake Hotel with Wallion. William Robertson has been set at liberty ere this, and would, naturally, tell all he knows. In short," said the Doctor with bitterness, "there is no lack of witnesses who can swear that we went out on a trip whence we shall require no return tickets."

"Fudge," said Dixon again, "the ocean is large."

"Answer me one thing," interrupted the Doctor. "How is it our wireless has received no inquiries about the *Ariadne* from either incoming or outgoing vessels?"

"Oh, I don't know."

"Well, I can tell you: it is because we are being tracked, and it was probably known that same evening that we were on board her. As they don't seem to be making inquiries about the yacht, I conclude they know all about her, that very likely a patrol-boat is chasing us already; and if they have discovered our final destination they will make straight for Hurricane Island and as likely as not arrive there before us."

A mournful silence followed this speech.

"I should say you're right about that," said Dixon.

"I'll just have a talk with the captain."

He was back again in five minutes.

"Hawkins says that with this wind the *Ariadne* can be at Hurricane Island by Wednesday evening, if I will take the risk of the boiler bursting," he said evidently greatly relieved.

"Well?" growled the Doctor.

"I said," continued Dixon, rather brutally, "I didn't mind if the *Ariadne* were shivered to atoms, provided he landed us safely on Hurricane Island by mid-day Wednesday, at the latest."

The Doctor, apparently satisfied, said nothing more, and, judging by the sound, the two men had turned back towards their cabins. Dixon had picked up the coat he had forgotten.

"Corman is no fool," remarked Wallion. "I was just going to say I wonder how far McTuft has got. When he gave up the black car, he very likely went back to the *Golden Snake*, where he would be told that the *Ariadne* had put out to sea. A patrol-boat would have been put at his disposal yesterday morning at latest, and a nice race it will be, indeed. I should rather like to give him a few choice bits of information...."

"Information as to what?" asked Tom.

"That there are always means of evasion," said Wallion suavely. "I only wish I had my faithful Browning."

"But tell me, do you think Captain Hawkins and the crew would come over to our side if we explained the situation to them?"

"H—m! I don't feel inclined to run the risk; my papers of identification are at the bottom of the sea near the Golden Snake Hotel, because I took off my shoes and coat when I swam out to the yacht. The coat I am wearing now I borrowed from the Captain's exceedingly well-stocked wardrobe." He laughed, but immediately became grave again. "No, my friend, if we were to show ourselves now, that precious 'Italian Detective' would have us shut up as members of the 'Black Hand.'" He pondered a while, and then remarked philosophically: "We must leave it to time, we have no particular inducement for interfering; besides, the *Ariadne* is taking us precisely where we want to go...."

"To Hurricane Island? I am not particularly keen on going there, especially in company with these gentlemen," replied Tom; "the place is so infernally out of the way too."

"That can't be helped," said Wallion, "business must always be settled in its proper place and at the proper time."

Soon the smoke from the tall, yellow funnel grew thicker and thicker, until it rolled in a compact black mass over the water. The vibration increased, and the noise of the propeller became louder; evidently the engines were working at the highest possible pressure. The strain had begun.

"Look here," said Wallion, much interested, "this abnormal speed shows the captain is keeping his word; by twelve o'clock the *Ariadne* will be lying at anchor off Hurricane Island."

* * * *

The yacht's wireless was installed behind the bridge and connected with the chart-house. Occasionally they caught a glimpse of the operator, a pale young man named Moreland. He had not much to do, and sometimes left his apparatus for an hour or two; consequently no messages were sent, and calls were left unanswered.

On the bridge, taking turns with Captain Hawkins, they noticed a young, smart-looking ship's officer, whom the captain addressed as "Weston." These two were evidently the only men in authority. Wallion took the crew to consist of five or six men only.

About 2 P.M., Tom experienced a sudden, most delightful thrill. Elaine Robertson appeared on deck; she was accompanied by Madame Lorraine, and the two walked up and down for nearly fifteen minutes, without uttering a word. Elaine seemed grave and worried; at every turn she stopped for a few seconds and looked wistfully towards the horizon. Did she hope she might see the smoke of a liner? Perhaps; but all around nothing was to be seen but passing clouds; and eventually she and Madame Lorraine went below. In the afternoon there was no one on the bridge.

Tom yawned; he was bored to death. He and Wallion had come to the end of their provisions. Night had fallen.

* * * *

After some hours of troubled sleep Tom awoke; the hard bottom of the boat was not exactly an ideal resting place; moreover, he was very hungry. It was still dark, but most of the night had passed and day was dawning in the East. He tried to look at his watch but could not see the hands; by his side Wallion continued fast asleep.

Two days and nights of enforced idleness had begun to tell on Tom. He did not like his unshaven chin; he was not accustomed—like his friend—to such small sacrifices on the altar of his profession; his muscles were stiff and his hunger astounding. If Wallion had been so successful in procuring food, why should not he?

The *Ariadne* sped through the darkness with no lights showing. Now and again Captain Hawkins might be seen walking to and fro on the bridge with long and resolute strides.

The pantry was only a little way off, and Tom supposed he might get there under cover. He determined to make the attempt.

The next time the Captain's steps turned to starboard, Tom leapt down on the deck and stole to the stairs; below, everything was dark and quiet. Automatically he counted the steps, of which there were eighteen, to the bottom, where the edge of a red carpet was visible. After some hesitation he stealthily walked down one step at a time, until he found himself standing on a red carpet. A corridor opened in front of him, and on either side were three closed doors; behind him, on the right of the stairs, was the saloon, and on the left a kind of store-room. He could see distinctly to the end of the corridor, thanks to a little electric lamp on the ceiling, and he noticed a door which he supposed would lead to the fore-part of the ship. With noiseless steps he made for it, but when he was about half-way along the corridor he had to put out his hands to save himself from falling. He had caught his foot in a piece of string which he could not shake off, and an electric bell close by was ringing, not loudly but continuously. A cold sweat broke out on his forehead. He made another desperate effort to free his foot, and broke the string.

The bell ceased to ring, but at the same moment three lamps in the ceiling flashed on. A door opened, and Doctor Corman stepped out, clad only in his pyjamas. He looked at Tom, and said with great deliberation:

"I see I was right; I suspected you were on board, and thought of proposing a search tomorrow. You are very welcome, Mr. Murner; there's a special cabin waiting for you."

Tom took a step forward, but a pair of strong arms gripped him from behind and held him as in an iron vice; it was Toroni. The owner of the yacht appeared at the same time, half-dressed, revolver in hand.

"What's up now?" said Dixon angrily. "Your alarm arrangement, Toroni, is the very ... Hallo!" he exclaimed as he caught sight of Tom, changing the pungent expletive he was going to use. He burst into a loud guffaw of satisfaction and surprise. "Well, who'd have thought it? *You* here? It's more than forty-eight hours since the *Ariadne* weighed anchor, and you have lain low until now ... Why so bashful? I trust you will not deprive us again of your pleasant company."

"It takes two for that," was Tom's infuriated answer.

He hurled himself with great violence upon Toroni, who missed his footing, uttered a vile oath, and losing hold of Tom, allowed him to slip between

Corman and Dixon, who knocked the revolver out of Dixon's hand in his mad rush for the stairs. Where he should go next he had not the least notion, but he thought his first and most important duty was to divert attention from Wallion and their place of concealment in the larboard boat. But his adversaries were too quick for him. On the lowest step he was stopped and seized by three pairs of hands. He struggled for a few minutes, but gave in when he found the muzzle of a pistol pointing at him.

"That's right, take things easy," said Dixon, in a tone bordering on friendliness. "We shall come to terms before long."

Tom breathed hard, but submitted to his fate in silence. Dixon looked up, listening intently. Tom feared that Wallion had betrayed himself by some impetuous movement in the boat, but Dixon was not looking in its direction. The wireless installation stood out against the bright, blue sky, and an intermittent crackling sound made itself plainly heard from above. Dixon ran up the stairs.

"What the devil are you doing, Moreland?" he shouted. "Are you mad?"

"Moreland is not here," answered the captain from the bridge. "He went to bed about eleven, Mr. Dixon."

The wireless had stopped short, Dixon looked up at the cables in anger and consternation.

"Who is sending a message?" he asked.

"Don't know," said the captain. "Weston says that two messages were sent during the night, we thought it might be Mr. Ferail."

"Confound it all," roared Dixon, white with fury. "Call out the crew, there is a spy on board."

A whistle sounded and the captain rushed up to the wireless room. Dixon pushed Tom back into the corridor, gave him a look which boded no good, and asked: "Who was with you?"

"I shan't tell you," Tom answered. He strongly suspected that Wallion had been in the wireless room, and he was fully determined not to admit anything.

"Was it McTuft?"

"No."

With a side glance at Toroni, Dixon said:

"Has a miracle happened? Was it Wallion?"

Tom moved impatiently.

"What's the use of asking me?" he said. "Do you believe I should be likely to give you any answer?"

Dixon, by this time more calm and sober, surveyed him attentively; his face wore an expression of cool determination.

"Shut him up in a safe place," he said to Corman and Toroni. Then he went on deck, and Tom heard him shout:

"Are you there, Weston? Take three men with you and search the boat thoroughly. Well, Captain Hawkins?"

"There's no one in the room, Mr. Dixon, but Moreland is there on duty now."

"All right, keep your eyes open, all of you…. A hundred dollars for the man who catches the spy. I shall expect to be face to face with him in half-an-hour…."

The voices sounded farther away. Toroni and the Doctor led Tom down the corridor. They unlocked a door on the starboard side, and signed to Tom to go in. The door was double-locked after him and he found himself shut in a narrow, but luxuriously furnished, cabin lighted by a lamp, with a yellow silk shade, fixed in the wall. He put out the lamp, for daylight already began to filter through the small port-holes, and forgetting his own pitiable plight he listened anxiously for what might be going on outside.

CHAPTER 20

ELAINE TELLS THE TRUTH

Tom heard orders given overhead and footsteps in all parts of the boat, but nothing to indicate that Wallion had been found. He had such unbounded faith in his friend's ingenuity and dexterity that he believed it quite possible that Wallion would succeed in escaping from his pursuers.

For a whole hour the noise continued to increase, then suddenly all was silent. A long way off, Dixon's voice could be heard, raised in anger. The Doctor seemed to be trying to soothe him. The two men were apparently going down the stairs.

Tom felt less anxious now. Clearly, in some unaccountable manner, Wallion had disappeared. He looked round his by no means horrible prison; behind some beaded drapery he discovered a small dressing-room, with hot and cold water laid on. There, too, he found a shaving kit, and managed to make quite a decent and comfortable toilet. Then he helped himself to a Virginia cigarette from a box of beaten copper and sat down with a sigh of resignation.

The *Ariadne* pursued her way, always at top speed; the black smoke cast long shadows on the water and the seething breakers beat against the little window.

About 10 A.M. the door opened, and a steward made an unexpected appearance.

"Mr. Dixon requests Mr. Murner's presence in the saloon," he said.

With mixed feelings Tom obeyed the summons. On entering he found Dixon, Corman and Toroni seated at a large table, and Hawkins standing before them.

"Well, Hawkins," said Dixon. "Here you see one of them, and if we can only catch the other we shall be all right. They are two of the most dangerous members of the 'Black Hand'...."

"That's a lie," broke in Tom angrily. "I am a Swede, and my name is Thomas Murner. Look here, here are my..." He was going to say "papers" but when he put his hand in his pocket he found they had gone; his pocket-book had been taken from him during the struggle in the corridor.

"Your *what*?" said Dixon derisively. "Your weapon? No, you are harm-less for the present, my friend. We found your hiding place in the larboard boat. Detective Ferail, my guest, has reason to be proud of his catch. Now tell us who your companion was, and where he has gone to?"

Tom bit his lip and said nothing. It was not worth while entering into any explanation with Hawkins, who, simple and honest seafaring man man as he was, surveyed him with some curiosity and distrust.

"So you won't answer?" continued Dixon. "You can go now, Captain, and resume the the search until the other fellow is found."

The captain took his leave. When he had gone Dixon burst out laughing. "You *do* look surprised, Mr. Murner; isn't our little joke to your taste? I am afraid it will be carried on a little longer though; but, no doubt, you understand that resistance can only lead to harder conditions, and make mat-ters worse for you, and that, with or without your consent, you must be our guest until the gold is hauled up. You see?" He gave Tom a cold and search-ing look.

"And then?" inquired Tom as calmly as he could.

"After that our ways will lie apart, you and your bashful, retiring friend will be sent on a little pleasure trip to ... shall we say ... Australia? Naturally, under the supervision of our good Hawkins."

Toroni remarked quietly:

"Much too much talk. I should have settled this business in a much sim-pler manner..."

"Misleading the police is quite enough," said Corman with evident dis-gust, and without looking at Toroni. "Our record is already sufficiently long."

One of the two doors Tom had noticed at the farther end of the saloon was thrown open, and Madame Lorraine with a cigarette between her lips walked in. She neither showed the least surprise nor took any notice of Tom, but turned to her brother and asked:

"Whatever is all the commotion on deck about?"

"There's some one on board we should rather like to get hold of," replied the Doctor. "You keep out of the way, it is nothing that concerns you."

Madame emitted a puff of smoke.

"Have you really searched everywhere?" she said with indifference. "Who can he be?"

"Well, we must see. There is no danger, but for safety's sake I just went in to have a look at Elaine. She seemed rather upset. You can comfort her, can't you?"

"Poor little thing," said Madame Lorraine, "I'll look after her..."

She threw the stump of her cigarette on an ash-tray and went out by the other door, closing it after her. Tom inferred that the cabins at the back of the saloon had been reserved for the two ladies.

"I suppose it is useless to put any more questions to you, Mr. Murner?" said Dixon after a pause.

"Perfectly useless."

"You won't even explain how you managed to come on board?"

"Certainly not."

"In that case I have only one piece of advice to give you. Hold your tongue and you won't have any complaint to make about your treatment here so long as you are my guest. Now, may I request you to return to your cabin? The steward will see that you have everything, except ... your liberty."

Tom turned on his heels and went back to his cabin. Ten minutes later, the waiter brought in a tray with a liberal breakfast. As he was eating Tom heard a quiet knock at the closed door. He looked at it in surprise. A white card had been pushed under it and lay on the floor. It was one of Wallion's visiting cards, and in the firm handwriting he knew so well, he read:

"Situation promising. Hold yourself in readiness. Our day is coming.—M.W."

Tom ran to the door and shook it, but there was no sound. He gently whispered Wallion's name; there was no response, but in a second or two the steward came up and asked from the outside:

"Did you require anything more, sir?"

"No, thank you, nothing," answered Tom. He flung himself down on the bed. Those few words on the card had been like refreshing wine to him. The blood mounted to his head, and his nerves tingled, but he was at a loss—turn or twist the words as he might—to account for such a message. Wallion's audacity, too, almost frightened him. How was all this to end?

Certain signs indicated that the *Ariadne* was approaching her journey's end, and Tom began to get fidgety. For safety's sake he tore the card to bits, which he threw out of a porthole. In the east, land could be discerned, and the boat, still at top speed, passed a number of islands, sometimes nearer, sometimes further away, gray and red, with dabs of dark woods.

Lunch was served at two o'clock, but Tom's appetite was gone.

"Shall we soon be there?" he asked.

"In about another hour," replied the steward civilly, but he beat a hasty retreat to avoid any further inquiries.

An hour went by. Tom walked restlessly up and down in his tiny cabin. Then bit by bit a high mountain ridge came in sight about a thousand yards away, and a little later, when the yacht had slackened speed, a steep arid coast in some parts covered with tall firs, and then a wide valley with lighter foliage in the background. The engines stopped, and the yacht anchored about a hundred yards from a dilapidated wooden pier. The *Ariadne* had reached her goal.

So this was Hurricane Island, and over there the "Black Valley"? On the left Tom noticed a jumble of sheds and chimneys.

The wharf mentioned was a very simple affair, there was no work going on, but a score of men came out on the quay, from mere curiosity. At some distance down the valley could be seen a skeleton swing-bridge, leading into a dark hole on the mountain side; this was the deserted copper mine; but, save for this reminder of bygone industry, the surrounding country was desolate.

A large motor boat came out from the quay, and when it got alongside the *Ariadne*, Tom noticed at the wheel a man who might have been the foreman of the wharf. He had evidently come to welcome his employers. The boat slipped round to the bow of the yacht and the Captain shouted from the bridge:

"Mr. Dixon is engaged, but lay to and come on board."

There was a high sea and the yacht rocked considerably. Things began to be very lively on deck and Tom wondered what was going on.

The steward came in hurriedly to remove the luncheon tray, and Tom had a shock.

This time the man had left the door unlocked! Tom listened, thinking he might come back. In the direction of the stairs, he heard Dixon's voice in sharp altercation with the Doctor.

"It is impossible," he was saying; "it can't be done now, the sea is too rough. We shall have to wait an hour or two."

"In an hour or two it may be too late," the Doctor replied.

"I don't think so. Besides it takes time to fix upon the exact place...."

"Well, and what about this Swede's friend whom we couldn't catch?"

"Haven't we thoroughly searched every nook and cranny? There wasn't a spot as big as a dollar left for any one to hide in. He isn't here, Corman. The wireless has given out, that is the solution of..." Their voices died away and they went up on deck.

Tom strained every nerve, trying to impress upon his memory the things he had heard; he conquered his desire to rush out, for Wallion's instructions had only been "keep himself in readiness." And Wallion was at liberty, probably with a deep scheme in his mind. Trembling with excitement he muttered, "Let us hope it won't be long ... if only I knew."

The yacht tugged at her cables, and Fir Island presently came in view. It was smaller and more wooded than Hurricane Island, and looked as if the foot of man had never trodden there.

The *Ariadne* lay about midway in the long and broad channel, through which the waters flowed freely, and there was still a high sea running, though the storm had abated; the clouds were heavy and twilight was falling. The motor boat was towing a low, flat-bottomed barge, laden with a variety of mysterious implements, towards some point which Tom was unable to see.

Immediately afterwards the yacht again weighed anchor and slowly proceeded in the same direction, stopped after backing a little, and again dropped anchor. Then feeble strokes became audible on the larboard side; the yacht was clearly alongside the barge.

A thought shot through Tom's brain. They were surely lying immediately over the wreck of the *King Solomon*. He felt he could no longer remain idle; in some way or another he must be doing. He opened the door and went into the corridor; the road was clear. Without any attempt to conceal his movements he walked straight into the saloon, where the lamps were already lighted, and there, by the table, with her back to the door, stood Elaine. Tom stopped short, but she had already heard him and now turned round. Her large, dark eyes sparkled, and a smile hovered round her trembling lips. She was grave yet excited.

"You?" she cried. "*You?*"

"Yes," he replied, taking her hands, "and you can't turn me out now," he added, half in jest. "We are still fellow-travelers, as you see, but it seems ages since I last talked to you."

Without withdrawing her soft hands from his she continued: "How dared you come on board the yacht?"

"You were the magnet, Elaine."

She blushed slightly, and her smile vanished; she looked furtively round.

"You ought not to have come..."

"Does my society bore you so much?"

"No, oh no, I am glad; you have done far too much for me already, I can never..."

"I do so want to be near you and be able to help you," he said, "if only you will tell me what I can do."

"No, you can't help me."

"It is true that I am but a sorry knight."

"I don't mean that, but don't you see, can't you understand, that it is too late? ..."

She pointed towards the table on which lay a number of sea-charts and drawings; the two wooden dolls had been carelessly thrown down among them.

"They have done their worst and we are entirely in their hands." Something in her tone made him lean towards her; her eyes burned with excitement and deep despair.

"Elaine," he asked impulsively, "you know all?"

"I do," she replied. "Oh, the scoundrels ... they deceived me, enticed me with lies ... my poor father ... Oh, Tom, it is too late..."

Almost unconsciously she had called him by his Christian name; tears rose to her eyes and she leant her head against his shoulder.

"What an idyllic scene!" said an ironical voice at the door. "I am afraid we are disturbing them, Dixon."

It was Doctor Corman and Dixon; on the threshold they stood still, an expression of scornful triumph on their faces.

"So we enticed you with lying words, Elaine?" said Corman mockingly. "What do you intend to do then, eh?"

"Shut up," said Tom, clenching his fists.

Corman pretended to be greatly surprised.

"So you have been pleased to leave your cabin, Mr. Murner? Oh, well, it is of no consequence."

Elaine had pulled herself together; the sight of the two men seemed to have put new vigor into her.

"Oh, yes, I know all about you, who choose a murderer for your friend and are worse than a thief yourself," she cried, in a loud, clear voice. "I overheard your conversation last night and am glad to be able to tell you the truth at last. Worse, yes, worse than a thief; compared with *you* a thief is an honest man, you who rob widows and orphans, plunder the dead and commit murder for the sake of gold. I see everything clearly now; I hope the truth will scorch your soul when you think of what you have done—you liar, you devil."

Corman's face twitched, and Dixon turned very white. After Elaine's accusing words there was a dead silence, till with a forced laugh Dixon said, rather hoarsely:

"Well, Miss Robertson, maybe you are right, only you have told us the truth just two months too late, and you can't stop us now..."

He looked around, but not at her. After some hesitation he passed in front of her and gathered up the papers from the table, looking at them with a covert smile.

"You see, my dear young lady, there are things in our miserable lives that you can't understand," he said.

Then he left the saloon in silence, and Corman went with him.

CHAPTER 21

TEN FATHOMS FROM THE GOAL

The wooden dolls still lay on the table, and as if in a dream, Tom noticed for the first time four other wooden figures on a shelf in the wall. A small marble clock on the same shelf gave forth six shrill, harsh strokes.

Elaine had sunk down on a seat on the larboard of the yacht, trembling nervously after her recent outbreak. Tom took a chair by her side; he wanted to say something to comfort her, but could not think of anything.

"Don't say anything," she whispered with a nervous little smile which ended in a shiver. "I am not going to be hysterical...."

Their attention was diverted by a noise and a light outside the window; they looked out, and saw that the barge had been towed alongside the yacht. Darkness lay over the sea, which had become much less turbulent. The searchlight turned obliquely on the long, low deck of the barge and its milk-white rays shone upon a curious spectacle. Preparations for hauling up *King Solomon*'s golden cargo were in full swing. A grotesque and clumsy gray figure, its feet weighted with lead, was walking along the planks; it was the diver. An assistant held the copper helmet in readiness, the breathing-tube was coiled round his body and a third man was looking after the air-pump. On the deck stood Dixon, Corman, and Toroni—the two former smoking in gloomy silence; the young girl's words must surely have burnt themselves into their consciences and embittered their hour of triumph.

Toroni, on the other hand, was watching the work with apathetic curiosity, self-centered, awaiting the result of the plot he had engineered with violence and cunning twelve months before; the hour when his hands should close on the coveted six millions. Did he really intend his two accomplices to have a share in the booty? Tom noticed the sinister look he cast at the others through his half-closed eyes. Was his subtle brain evolving another piece of villainy? The expression of his face seemed to say, "I am quite aware that you despise me, though you have no objection to share the roast ... but don't be too sure." He walked up to them, pointed to the water, and with a cynical grimace said a few words.

Tom noiselessly opened the ventilator and distinctly heard Corman's answer:

"And then? If they can't find it there, we are lost, that's all about it." He made a weary and deprecating gesture with his hands.

"But it is there," said Toroni, in a low voice. "Sixteen years ago I saw it disappearing in the sea on the very spot upon which we are standing today ... Why don't you say something? ... Why don't you laugh?" and once more he pointed to the dark, rolling waves. "Only ten fathoms from the prize," he whispered, "only ten fathoms from *King Solomon* ... haven't you anything to say?"

Dixon turned his back upon him in order to make an end of the matter, at the same time shouting to the diver:

"Ready there? ... Look sharp about it."

The diver went down the steps and into the water up to his waist; he hitched an electric lamp with brightly polished reflector on to his chest, and the helmet was screwed on over his head. The air-pump began to work with long, absorbent puffs, and the copper helmet gradually disappeared under the water, which bubbled up over it; the assistant paid out the coil and the rope with mechanical precision. Fifteen minutes passed, then the diver came up again on the steps. Toroni bent down to him, and Dixon and Corman also came forward; the diver opened the little glass pane in the helmet.

"The wreck is there all right; it has sunk a little lower, but there are no difficulties. The chests are all right in the saloon."

"The fifteen, all told?" inquired Toroni.

"Yes, all of them, safe and uninjured."

Toroni gave his friends a look, but no word passed between them. A windlass had been rigged up over the side of the barge, and the diver at once went back to the wreck, taking a supple steel wire with him.

The group on the boat stood stiff and motionless in silent expectation; the men looked like coal-black shadows in the steady rays of the searchlight; it was pitch dark all round. Tom, sick with suspense, sought the back of a chair as support. Everything had gone so fast and in such a business-like manner that time after time he was forced to repeat to himself: "The gold is there, it is there."

Again, in despair, he asked: "Where can Wallion be, what can prevent him from coming?"

CHAPTER 22

MADAME LORRAINE'S SURPRISE

There were suspicious movements in the saloon behind them, and Elaine uttered a cry. It was Madame Lorraine, but a greatly changed Madame Lorraine; her sea-green eyes shone with a peculiar emotion, and she looked at them both with an expression that made Tom hurriedly get up from his chair. She went close up to him and put a revolver into his hand.

"You are stout-hearted," she said in so low a voice that he could scarcely hear her. "Your friend says the time has come; take this, it is loaded ... I have always kept it by me as a last resource."

He hardly understood her.

"What do you mean?" he said.

"Do not speak so loud," she answered. "It was I who slipped the card under your door, I have a surprise in store for you ... and *them*," she added, in still more subdued tone. Through the ventilator she cast a look of intense hate upon the silent group outside.

Then Tom grasped the fact that Madame Lorraine had deserted her associates and come over to the enemy! He remembered that her conduct throughout had often puzzled both Wallion and himself. Now she had come to a decision, driven thereto by the loathsome presence of Toroni. The cabin occupied by Madame Lorraine had been the only place not subjected to the rigorous search made for the "Problem Solver."

With one bound Tom dashed through the half-open door into Madame Lorraine's cabin ... there, at the table, stood Maurice Wallion, in the act of loading a revolver.

"I am just coming," he said, looking over his shoulder and smiling. "You know, it was rather cute of you to let yourself be caught this morning," he added, coming out into the saloon. "You see, I had sent a few wireless messages to McTuft during the night, but obviously that could not go on much longer; and when that big raid was on I had the good luck to find Madame Lorraine alone here in the saloon, so I persuaded her to come to a noble and reasonable decision" (here he made a polite little bow). "Thanks for your hospitality, Madame, it will never be forgotten," he said. Then he shot a keen glance through the window and frowned.

"The time has come," he said abruptly, "they are much too busily engaged out there to suspect our plans."

"What plans are those?"

"To take possession of the yacht."

Tom was just as eager for action as his friend. "Yes," he said, almost breathless with excitement, "go on, you'll have me near you."

They left the ladies in the saloon and hurriedly went out.

"Where is McTuft?" asked Tom.

"He is chasing us in the *Albatross*, a patrol-boat; and, acting on my instructions, he will be here soon."

Tom's confidence in Wallion rose many degrees at that piece of information. He had no doubt that they could have surprised the conspirators without assistance, but to deliver them up to the law was a more ticklish affair; for that purpose McTuft and his "boys" would prove very useful.

They looked about them for a few minutes from the top of the gangway. On the larboard side lay the barge, well-lighted up by the rays of the searchlight, whilst all was dark and still on the yacht. The crew stood leaning over the railings, looking on with great interest; on the bridge near the wireless hut were Captain Hawkins and the pilot Weston. Tom accompanied Wallion along the dark deck to the bridge. Scattered lights from the wharf were reflected in the water, but there was no danger to be apprehended from that quarter.

"Moreland is in the wireless room," said Wallion. "When we get there you must go straight up to him and point your revolver at his head. I shall persuade the captain and pilot to go in there too; the rest I will take into my own hands."

They stole up to the bridge like a couple of cats, only stopping occasionally to take breath.

The well-lighted wireless room was just behind the chart-house; and immediately in front, on the other side of the steering-wheel, they saw the unmistakable silhouettes of Hawkins and Weston.

The rhythmic suction of the air-pumps and the sharp creaking of the windlass could be heard far and wide in the stillness of the night.

"Now then, go ahead," said Wallion.

Tom straightened himself and noiselessly entered the hut. Moreland looked up, and turned pale when he saw the revolver pointed at his head.

"Sit still," said Tom, in a commanding tone; "if you move I fire."

The telegraphist sat as motionless as a stone image.

Meanwhile Wallion crept up behind Hawkins and Western.

"Gentlemen," he said, "this is no time for talking; I shall fire without compunction, if necessary. Go to the wireless room at once in front of me."

They obeyed with hands up, and he ordered them to sit down with their hands in front of them. Then he locked the door.

"Now for a little explanation," he said with a smile. "I regret having to act in this cavalier fashion, but I had to make you hear what I have to say, without raising an alarm; you take us for two bandits belonging to the Black Hand gang, don't you?"

"Mr. Dixon said so," retorted the captain sullenly.

"Very well, listen now; Mr. Dixon told a downright damned lie. My name is Maurice Wallion, and I am a detective from Sweden, and this gentleman" (pointing to Tom) "is my friend and assistant, Mr. Murner."

Captain Hawkins stared distrustfully at him. "Anybody might say that," he growled.

"But I can swear that it *is* so."

"In that case there should be no difficulty in proving your identity."

"My own papers have been lost, and Murner's have been taken away from him."

The captain shook his head. "Excuse me if I don't believe you; besides, what business could you have on board Mr. Dixon's yacht?"

"My business here is to arrest Ricardo Ferail for murder and theft, and Dixon and Corman for aiding and abetting," Wallion said very quietly.

Captain Hawkins stared as if he had heard something perfectly impossible. "You're a good 'un," he said scornfully, "you can tell that tale to the marines."

"Then you don't believe what I say?"

"I don't."

Tom cast a troubled look at Wallion; it seemed to him the situation was becoming critical.

"It will afford me much pleasure to prove every word I have said, Captain Hawkins."

"How are you going to do that? ... It would be rather amusing," was Hawkins' answer.

"It will be very simple: a few nautical miles from here is an American patrol-boat, the *Albatross*, with Detective McTuft from Seattle on board. He knows me well, and is, like myself, on the track of the same delightful trio."

"Oh," said the captain, with growing interest.

"What could be easier than to make an inquiry by wireless, requesting McTuft to prove our identity?"

The captain rose, but immediately sat down again. "Not impossible," he said at last, "Moreland, call up the *Albatross*, then we shall hear."

Wallion exchanged a look of triumph with Tom, but their present position was rather hazardous all the same. The operator bent over his apparatus, whilst the others kept silent; he called up the *Albatross*, and waited for an answer. It came at once:

"Who wants *Albatross*?"

"Maurice Wallion, on board the *Ariadne*, replied Moreland. "Ask McTuft if he will, please, come to the apparatus.""

"So far I have told you the truth, you see," remarked Wallion, while they were waiting for the reply. "I presume fire-arms will no longer be needed."

"No," replied the Captain, curtly; "but I mean to get to the bottom of this," he said, adding: "if you have told the truth and anybody down there in the barge heard you, this room may prove a dangerous place for you."

"There is no danger; the air-pump and windlass drown the wireless, and what is more, their attention is entirely taken up with those gold chests."

Moreland made a sudden movement as the reply came: "McTuft is here, go ahead, *Ariadne*."

"Will you speak, Captain, or shall I?" said Wallion.

He and Tom laid aside their arms as being no longer required. Captain Hawkins was deeply interested, and said:

"Let me, please, Mr. Wallion." Then he proceeded to dictate his message to Moreland: "Request McTuft to furnish us with a description of Wallion."

Moreland sent it off immediately, and after a scarcely perceptible delay a prompt answer came through space: "Maurice Wallion, detective from Sweden; tall, thin, eyes gray, complexion dark, hair brushed back from forehead; has Thomas Murner with him, do you want HIS description as well?"

Whilst the captain was hesitating about the next inquiry to make, further signs of life arrived from McTuft; he asked: "What's the matter with Wallion? Anything gone wrong?"

"No, nothing," dictated Hawkins, gloomily; "only that he wants to impress upon the *Ariadne*'s company that certain proceedings are unavoidable; send information regarding his business on board the yacht for registration."

The reply, a very emphatic one, came at once; one might have fancied it was in McTuft's own indignant tones: "It is Wallion's business to arrest every single soul on board the *Ariadne*, if they make a fuss; first and foremost the owner and his party; will that do for you?"

"That's enough," said Hawkins, and laughed; then he added rather seriously: "I am quite convinced now, Mr. Wallion. It is an unsavory, horrible story, and my own plight is most deplorable; but, of course, I must bow to the law. What do you wish me to do?"

"That depends" ... said Wallion. He turned to Moreland and dictated as follows: "It is I, Wallion, speaking. Thanks for information, how long before the *Albatross* will reach Hurricane Island?"

Out of the darkness came McTuft's reply: "Thanks to you for information given last night; the *Albatross* will be up in half-an-hour." There the odd conversation ended. Wallion got on to his feet and laughingly remarked to Tom:

"I begin to appreciate McTuft's tenacity. He has no intention of missing the last act of the tragedy. I fancy I see him now on the *Albatross*."

He put his head out of the window for a moment. The work on the barge below was being carried on undisturbed; the pumps moaned and the windlass creaked at regular intervals.

"Are the crew to be trusted?" asked Wallion.

"Yes, if I may have the handling of them," answered the captain.

The pilot undertook to call the men in one by one and to explain the circumstances to them.

"Yes, that would perhaps be the best," Wallion agreed; "what is your opinion about the five men on the barge?"

"They belong to the wharf and they will give no trouble," said the captain. "I don't think any of the workmen on the wharf are particularly delighted with their employers."

"First rate. I propose that you will call your men to the chart-room and tell them to be quiet; it is not necessary for them to interfere. Dixon and his two associates are armed, but we shall get the better of them before they have finished their business down there."

All except Moreland left the cabin.

"Tom," said Wallion in a low voice, "in about ten minutes there will be a nice scuffle; you keep an eye on the barge whilst I help the captain to prepare the crew, and come up to the chart-room if any of our three friends make as though they meant to return to the yacht."

Tom leant over the rails on the bridge and looked down into the barge; he felt that never again in all his life would he find himself in such company or such a situation as this. He was calm and resolute, and his gaze was firmly fixed on what lay before him.

CHAPTER 23

GO SHARES ... THEN PART

The rays of the searchlight fell upon the deck of the barge, on the rude planks of which a strange scene was being enacted, In the background lay Fir Island, like a dark side-piece, and the water in the channel rose and fell in glittering, heaving billows. On the stage, below where Tom stood, were eight performers all told.

Dixon and Corman, in the center of the barge and still motionless, were smoking, and had lighted their cigarettes without exchanging a word; Toroni sat on the railing as close as possible to the spot where the ever-seething air bubbles in the water indicated the place where the diver was working on the wreck sixty feet below. Two men attended to the air-pumps, one looked after the tube and signal-rope, and two others stood ready by the stake, from which wire ropes hung down into the deep.

But the picture had undergone a marvelous change since Tom had watched it from the loophole in the saloon. A collection of wooden cases of dark and curious appearance had been deposited on planks in a pool of muddy water. These cases were almost square and provided with thick iron bands; the offside of each showed letters carefully incised. Tom thought he could detect the name "Craig Russel" on one of the chests.... They contained gold from the ill-fated *King Solomon*, which, after sixteen years, had at last come up from the bottom of the sea.

He counted the chests and had got as far as ten when the man in charge of the signal-rope raised his hand; the two on duty at the stake rushed over the tackling to the edge of the boat, and half a minute later, the eleventh chest was hauled up over the railing and placed by the side of the others; then the wire rope slackened.

Toroni bent over this last chest and closely examined it on all sides. Like the others it was sound and uninjured; made of good, stout oak, the chests were in a wonderful state of preservation, though the wood had turned nearly black and the iron bands had been eaten away by rust and came off in bits. Apparently satisfied, Toroni returned to his post of observation in silence; his two companions had not stirred.

The diver down on the wreck seemed working with a will, and ere long the twelfth case made its appearance. There were three more to come up, and Toroni and his accomplices had all but attained their object.

There was something rather ghastly in the grim silence observed by these three, within reach of the coveted six millions they had agreed to share. What was it that so deeply engrossed their thoughts at this moment?

Tom was inclined to believe that he could pretty well guess what was in Dixon's mind; he meant to have the gold conveyed to the big motorboat from the wharf and to smuggle it over the frontier into Canada, before abandoning the *Ariadne* with Elaine, Tom, and the other intruders on board. There was every prospect of such a plan proving successful, provided nothing occurred to nip it in the bud, but ... did that plan fit in with Toroni's calculations?

Tom narrowly scrutinized that little man's ill-favored countenance with its black beard, shifty eyes and pale brow; he appeared no longer to worry about Dixon or Corman, his eyes swept the water's which concealed *King Solomon*.

Chests thirteen and fourteen also were safely transferred to the barge; water flowed over the planks freely, and masses of seaweed were thrown up all around.

Tom looked uneasily at the clock. Wallion had said ten minutes, but already twenty had elapsed. He turned his head; deliberations still seemed to be going on in the hut; he could distinguish the captain's broad back, Wallion's clear-cut profile and the pilot's anxious features; the last of the sailors had left and gone down. Tom turned his eyes to the deck; the crew had disappeared, but inquisitive eyes peered from the forecastle. The men were evidently prepared.

All at once the door of the hut was pushed open, and Wallion came out, followed by Hawkins and Weston, pocketing their fire-arms.

The windlass creaked for the fifteenth time ... the last remnant of *King Solomon*'s cargo was on its way up. Wallion looked down, his sharp features had assumed a hard, resolute expression.

"Just right," he said. "You, Mr. Weston, had better go down and keep an eye on the men and will you, Captain Hawkins, please remain on the bridge. You and I, Tom, will move a little nearer to our fellow-travelers down there."

Noiselessly they climbed down to the *Ariadne*'s lower deck, then made their way along under the bridge which brought them within five yards of Dixon and Corman, who were standing with their backs turned to the yacht, not suspecting anything. Toroni was just getting on his feet again after a minute inspection of the fifteenth and last chest, which stood dripping beside the others. The diver came up and climbed over the side of the barge; his helmet was unscrewed and the air-pump ceased working.

All was quiet. Toroni turned to his two friends.

"None of them have been damaged," he said, in a voice which ended in a hoarse whisper. "Look sharp now, it's all done.... Let's get away with the stuff as fast as we can. Quick."

Dixon sighed as if he were just waking from a bad dream. He threw away the stump of his cigarette, turned his head in the direction of the bridge and shouted: "Captain Hawkins, give the signal for the motorboat to come here."

The Captain neither moved nor spoke, but Wallion leveled his revolver.

"No signal is required, Dixon," he answered, "everything is arranged."

Dixon and Corman swung round and stared Wallion full in the face.

The Doctor muttered an oath and felt for his pocket. Wallion and Tom looked at him fixedly, and the former said:

"Don't add another to the list of your crimes; that would be foolish."

Dixon's lips had assumed an ashen hue, and he had evidently to make a tremendous effort to stand steady.

"Oho, so it was you, Mr. Wallion," he said with some bitterness in his tone. "Well, I give in, I have got into deep water. Corman, my boy, it wasn't written in the stars that this was the way we were to get rich...." Then, looking at Wallion, he said: "And what do you intend to do with us?"

"You are my prisoner, Dixon, and you too, Corman. Go shares and then dissolve partnership, that was your program, wasn't it? Well, the six millions will be shared, but not with you, and the partnership will be dissolved, though not quite in the way you intended."

Toroni, whom Wallion had kept well under observation, stood as if glued to the spot, his piercing black eyes fixed on the "Problem Solver."

The five bargemen and the diver were huddled together in a frightened heap. Toroni looked round.

"Don't expect you'll get any help," said Wallion sternly. "Come here, Toroni.... What? ... You would? ... Look out, Tom."

Quick as lightning Toroni had taken refuge behind the gold chests, pulled out his revolver and fired; the bullet made a hole in the wall of the hut. Wallion stooped and took aim, but he could not sight his adversary. Tom caught a glimpse of Toroni's right hand as he again raised his weapon between two of the chests and fired at random without any particular aim. A flash and a bang followed; Tom felt something like the sting of a whip on his left temple. He put up his hand; his fingers were wet and smeared with blood. He let fall his Browning and believed he heard himself call out: "I am wounded"; but in reality no sound passed his lips. He took a few steps without knowing where he was going, staggered and fell forward unconscious.

Toroni had dropped on his knees. He was grinning and showing his teeth like a wild beast. Under cover of the gold chests, he shot time after time at Wallion, who promptly returned the fire, and knew he had not missed his mark, but Toroni seemed possessed of an evil spirit.

"Give in," shouted Wallion. "I want to take you alive."

Toroni rose to his full height and threw away his weapon; he had fired his last shot. In his eyes there was the look of an untamed tiger.... Furious anger at the loss of what he thought already safe within his sordid grasp, lust of the millions upon which his thoughts had centered through sixteen years, had obliterated every trait of humanity.

"Never," he said huskily; he took a step forward.... A long, sharp knife gleamed in his hand as he raised it towards Wallion. At the same instant Madame Lorraine's voice was heard:

"You devil! It was you who dragged us down to perdition."

She had come to the railing of the yacht and picked up Tom's revolver. She looked as if she were intent on fulfilling a long neglected duty. She fired.... Toroni dropped the knife and reeled backwards, his failing eyes still sought the gold chests, then he folded his hands upon his breast, turned, staggered against the side of the barge, and blindly stretching out his arms, fell into the water. As his body sank, great bubbles rose to the turbid surface; the thirteenth passenger of the *King Solomon* had returned to where the gold had lain which lured him to his fate. Madame Lorraine silently retired to her cabin.

Dixon and Corman had looked on at the short but unforgettable scene with indifference and apathy. Their parts were played and they had neither the power nor the will to offer any resistance to the law.

Weston and two of the sailors went on board the barge and conveyed the two friends to the upper deck of the *Ariadne*. They moved listlessly, like automatons, and Dixon sank wearily into one of the basket-chairs. He buried his head in his hands and, looking up at Wallion's approach, said feebly:

"I suppose jail will be our next destination, Mr. Wallion?"

The latter nodded and said nothing. He rather pitied Dixon, whose gray and crestfallen features had aged in a few days by ten years.

Doctor Corman stood behind him, stoical and resigned, with folded arms. "Ah, well," he muttered. "Toroni came off best after all."

By Wallion's orders Tom had been carried down into the saloon. The young man had only a flesh-wound, and that a slight one, on one of his temples; but the shock had stunned him and he was still unconscious.

As soon as Wallion had satisfied himself that his friend was not in danger, he returned to the upper deck. He had heard distant signals across the water. The lights of a steamer soon became visible in the channel. She was approaching at full speed. It was the *Albatross*, with McTuft on board, his red hair blowing round his head like flames of fire.

"Hallo, Wallion," lie cried, "are things all right, or have I come too late?"

"You have come in the nick of time," was Wallion's answer, "to take these fifteen chests, which contain gold, on board the *Albatross*, and set the police seal on them. There you see Mr. Dixon and Doctor Corman; it is now your duty to arrest them. We shall remain on the *Ariadne* with Captain Hawkins to take us back to Seattle. That's all, I think...."

"But what about Ferail?"

"Ferail, otherwise No. 13 Toroni, is dead."

McTuft cast a long inquiring look at Wallion.

"If only you were a Scotchman now proud I should be of you," he said.

CHAPTER 24

AFTER THE CONFLICT

When Tom regained consciousness, it was with the feeling that his body was lying at full length in a swing and that a screw was being driven into his head. He heard the clank of chains and the starting of machinery. His memory came back by slow degrees. A snapshot in black and white representing the deck of the barge, figures moving and smoke curling up in thick clouds floated across his brain. "Yes, of course, I have been wounded," he thought confusedly.

And then something even more strange occurred, and that quite close to his side. Someone was breathing hard and saying in a broken voice:

"Wake up, dearest, look at me, and say that you are not in danger, my dear one, my love." ... Two soft, warm lips were pressed on his, then shyly withdrawn, only to return in a passionate kiss. It was indeed marvelous!

"I expect I am dreaming," he thought as he opened his eyes.

Elaine's tear-stained, lovely face was very near to his, an expression of unspeakable anxiety and distress in her eyes. He raised himself upon his elbow and put a hand up to his head; it was tightly bandaged.

"Won't you say once more what you said just now?" he murmured, rather incoherently.

She bent her head and blushed.

"It is all over now," she said softly; "Dixon and Corman are prisoners, and Toroni is dead; it was he who fired at you, and oh ... I am so glad that the wound is not dangerous."

Tom fell back against the cushions. He had discovered that he was lying on the couch in the saloon and they were alone.

"I don't know," he said, hesitating. "I fancy it might be most dangerous unless I have a kind and loving nurse."

"I shall try to do my best," she replied in a gentle tone.

He sat up with a bound and drew her to him.

"Elaine," he said, "I love you."

She lay still in his arms; he raised her head and kissed her. "I have loved you from the first moment I saw you," he said.

She smiled faintly. "That's an old, old story which you can read in any book."

"Yes, I know that. I only said it as the correct thing and as a matter of form. But really, Elaine, I have loved you from the time when you were recovering from the fever of your wound, and I saw you at the window in my smoking-room. My darling, say once more what you said just now when I opened my eyes."

She bent down, looked into his eyes, and said: "I love you."

"No, say it in Swedish," he said in a tone of command.

"*Jag älskar dig*," she repeated obediently.

* * * *

A month later, Maurice Wallion was sitting in a chair facing the Chief of the Secret Service Division of New York in his private office. They were smoking the cigars the Chief had once mentioned on the telephone, and he was listening with intense interest to Wallion's graphic story.

"Well, and what do you think of McTuft?" he said genially when the story was finished.

"A fine, intelligent fellow, but as obstinate as a mule," replied Wallion, laughing. "I strongly recommend him for promotion."

The Chief sat quiet for a time, turning over in his mind the tale he had just heard.

"It will be a perplexing business to discover all those heirs and share out the gold properly."

"A local Seattle paper is going to take the initiative and form a sort of Managing Committee," said Wallion, "but William Robertson was not anxious that all the world should know about it and, I suppose, the higher powers will also have a word to say in the matter."

"Naturally. By the way, I conclude you will not be present when Dixon and Corman come up for trial?"

"No, I have other business in hand, but I left with the Public Prosecutor a clear and full account of my part in the affair. In a way, I am rather sorry for Dixon: his power and influence were in reality only nominal ... he coveted wealth and position, and was dragged down against his better knowledge. As to Madame Lorraine, she is sure to be acquitted, for she was entirely under her brother's sway. But Doctor Corman deserves and must expect severe punishment; he knew well enough what he was doing."

"Yes," said the Chief Detective, meditatively, "we humans are a queer lot to be called the 'crowning piece' of creation. And the nice little lady ... Elaine Robertson, what promises does the future hold out to her?"

"Elaine Murner, once Robertson, you mean; she is very well, judging from Tom's jubilant telegram despatched immediately after the wedding. Her father is coming over to Sweden to take up his abode with Christian Dreyel. Elaine, of course, will be with her happy—architect husband...."

For a time they continued to smoke without speaking, then the Chief asked:

"Now, as to your own plans, Wallion: the man who saved *King Solomon*'s millions has a right to a good big reward."

But Maurice Wallion interrupted him, and stooping, unlocked a Gladstone bag which lay at his feet. Extracting therefrom twelve brown wooden dolls, he set them in a row on the table, and said with a laugh:

"As a reward I claim these ... as a souvenir of

NO. 13 TORONI."

www.ingramcontent.com/pod-product-compliance
Lightning Source LLC
Chambersburg PA
CBHW011447170626
46816CB00008B/2556